THE FAKE GAME

THE FAKE GAME

ANTHONY FOWLES

GREENWICH EXCHANGE
LONDON

This is a work of fiction and any resemblance to actual persons, living or dead, is purely coincidental.

Greenwich Exchange, London

First published in Great Britain in 2022
All rights reserved

The Fake Game © Anthony Fowles 2022

This book is sold subject to the conditions that it shall not, by way of trade or otherwise, be lent, resold, hired out or otherwise circulated without the publisher's prior consent in any form of binding or cover other than that in which it is published and without a similar condition including this condition being imposed on the subsequent purchaser.

Printed and bound by imprintdigital.com
Cover design: December Publications
Tel: 07951511275

Greenwich Exchange Website: www.greenex.co.uk

Cataloguing in Publication Data
is available from the British Library

Cover art courtesy of Shutterstock

ISBN: 978-1-910996-58-4

1

THE PERSONALITY TV HOST WAS ALL eyes, teeth and prefabricated cue-carded comment. The condescending camaraderie was broadcast fairly evenly between the programme's alleged contestants and the camera lens. In due succession she stood alongside each participant's easel and courtesy of a series of banal and predictable questions enabled each painter to bask in the limelight of stating the obvious about his or her handiwork.

'Who do you think is going to come out the winner?' Ethan Shaw asked from the comfort of the long, low, grey sofa and Virginia Faulkner's cuddling embrace.

'Well,' she said, 'given that What's-her-face has told us that sixty per cent of the point count will be made up of viewers' telephone votes, I would say that trollop with the excessive cleavage from whatever that soap is should walk away with it.'

'Wobble away with it, you mean,' Ethan Shaw said. 'Heaven forfend it, but you're probably right. The one who should win is that slim, dark woman. That still-life she's produced is mind-blowing. Realism? Abstract? You tell me. Cezanne would have given his right arm to have knocked that out.'

'Which might have cramped his style a bit.'

'Ho, ho. Who is she anyway?'

'Not exactly sure. Does the weather from time to time, I think.'

'She's in the wrong line of work. She's seriously more than some trendy Sunday – ' Cutting his sentence short with its abrupt unexpectedness the landline phone rang. Disengaging herself with minimum fuss, Virginia Faulkner rose to her feet and by the third ring had picked up. Ethan Shaw could make out a man's voice getting into its stride at the far end as it tried to sell wine or initiate a scam.

'Oh yes! Of course I remember,' Virginia said, 'Hello. How are you?'

The voice went on. Who then?

'Good,' Virginia said. 'And we're both fine, thank you. Never better.' The voice said something short and then something quite long.

'That's because he's here,' Virginia said. 'In all his glory. I'll pass you over to him.'

She stood up straight, tall and elegant over the glass coffee table on which the receiver had rested, and cupped her hand over its mouthpiece.

'It's that Detective Inspector Bradley,' she said. 'Careful what you say.'

Still sitting, craning forward, he took over the phone.

'Hello, Alec,' he said. 'How are you? How's things?'

'Things are ... interesting,' DCI Alec Bradley said in his estuary English voice, lustreless and thin at the far end of the line. 'I tried you at yours and then realised this might be the better bet.'

'These days it is, yes. What can I do for you?'

'A couple of things have come up. I was hoping we could have a meet. Strictly off the record.'

'Yes, that would be nice,' Ethan said without a moment's hesitation. 'Over a beer, maybe.'

'What I had in mind too. You remember The Swan?'

' ... er ... '

'Just on from Deptford High Street.'

'Oh yes, of course. Bit of a schlep from Hammersmith.'

'But close to home if you're ever there these days.'

'True ... well, that can be arranged.'

'How about next Thursday evening? The seventeenth?'

'Er ... can't see why not. No, that would be fine.'

'About eight, eh?'

'Yes. No problem. What's on your mind?'

'Better discussed face to face. Tell you then.'

'OK. Mine's a pint of Ordinary.'

'Ordinary it will be.' Click! As abruptly as it had arrived the call was terminated. Ethan handed the phone back up to the still standing Virginia. She was looking down at him anxiously.

'What is it?' she asked.

'Well, as you probably clocked, he wants to meet up for a chat. Off the record, as he puts it.'

'Oh. What about?'

'Too sensitive for the phone, it seems.'

She still looked anxious.

'They've believed our version so far,' she said.

'Yes.'

'Think I should come along too?'

Ethan considered the idea for some lengthy seconds.

'Probably not, Ginny,' he said finally. 'Probably a case of safety in lack of numbers.'

It must have been the best part of six months since Ethan

Shaw had had a drink in The Swan with DCI Alec Bradley. A lot of blood had flowed under the bridge since then. Now, however, as he shoved on through the stiff door that opened directly from the pavement outside, it seemed that for an instant that time had been standing still. What seemed the same crowd of extras sourced from Central Casting, some dozen or so, continued to populate the long, thin single bar in self-contained clusters of twos and threes. There at the far end of the counter in what Ethan had already recognised to be his usual spot, stood an unchanged Alec Bradley. Hang about! Something had changed. Bradley had a drinking partner with him this time. A woman. Smiling his recognition, he advanced towards them and Ethan found himself speculating what sort of a dark horse's private life Bradley kept hidden beneath his drab and faded exterior. Yes, ten years or so the younger, the lady looked to be a perfect stable companion for an honest, aging copper. But watch it! There was nothing faded about Bradley's wits! Ethan polished up his initial smile and thrust out his hand.

'Alec,' he said, 'good to see you.'

They shook hands and even as he did so Bradley was sliding an already pulled pint along the counter with his left hand.

'Got one in for you,' he said. 'I'll drink it myself if you'd prefer a short.'

'No, this what I ordered. Cheers!'

'Cheers!'

His throat and mouth were quite dry. He needed a pint. Nerves, no doubt. As he swallowed he looked at the policeman over the rim of his glass. No, no immediate change there: the same almost colourless raincoat, the same tie, the same suit worn down to anonymity. He shifted his eyes sideways and Bradley picked up on the cue.

'Ethan,' he said. 'My manners. Let me introduce a colleague. DI Jean Stafford. Jean, meet Ethan Shaw.'

'Oh yes,' she said. 'The painter. Alec's told me a bit about you.'

What bit, he wondered, as they nodded to each other.

'Wanna-be painter,' he said. 'I'm not so long out of Art School.'

'Yes, Goldsmiths, I understand,' she said. 'Just up the road.'

She had a pleasant, even refined, way of speaking – several notches up the social scale from Bradley's. She might well have passed as Ginny's somewhat older sister – tall, her longish face agreeably symmetrical, her mouth decisively wide. Her dark hair was straight, with a side parting and grown out to below her ears. He gave her points that she had made no attempt to dye the few streaks of grey that had begun to qualify the black.

It might be an idea to get on some kind of front foot. He looked past Jean Stafford and then back at her.

'Might it be an idea to sit down?' he said.

'It certainly would,' Jean said, smiling her thanks. 'I've spent all day pounding corridors.'

They gravitated to the small table his glance had picked out.

'So what shall we drink to?' Bradley said. 'How about "Coincidence"?'

'Coincidence?'

'Yes. The coincidence of us meeting in a pub so near to your old college and within striking distance of your flat.'

'Well, hardly a coincidence given that you particularly arranged we should meet up right here and now.'

'True. Not so much a coincidence as the fact that a rather sensational homicide incident took place within walking distance of that said flat and the two deceased both turning out to be persons you'd become intimately involved with prior to their ending up stretched out on the heath just down the road with their toes turned up.'

Ethan felt his stomach muscles tighten and then grow disturbingly slack. He was glad to be sitting down. 'Off the record' Bradley had promised on the phone: but even without a second DI sitting alongside, this would have been too close to home for comfort.

'A corrupt politician,' Ethan fought back with, 'and a known to be bent ex-cop meeting. When, the one attempted to use incriminating letters to blackmail the other, they both lost it big time and did each other in. As the inquest duly determined. As did all the national headlines too. Good riddance, I think the general feeling was.'

'Oh yes,' Jean said. 'A lot of files were closed on that one.'

'Good riddance, perhaps,' Bradley said, 'but even more of a strange coincidence is that at the time of the dual killings a third person, one explicitly mentioned in the letters found at the scene, was to be found having his portrait painted in that very flat of yours just that shortish stroll away.'

Bradley paused theatrically and reached forward to take a full swig from his pint with what seemed genuine gusto.

'It's not such a big thing these days to get an inquest verdict overthrown, you know,' he said.

Ethan responded in kind by taking a long, time-consuming pull on his own beer.

'Well,' he said eventually, 'were there to be another such inquest, I can assure you my testimony would be identical.'

'Why were you painting a portrait around midnight?' Jean asked. 'Is the light especially good at that time of night?'

You clever-dick astute bitch, Ethan thought. Quick!

'Stephen was working pub hours back then,' he almost immediately replied. 'It was damn near impossible to get hold of him. That was his day off. As I said in the witness box, I had to make the best of a bad job and make the most of what time I could get him for.'

'Thing is,' Bradley continued, 'a thing that was never really cleared up, is that one of the two, Reynolds, was shot in the back. By a Webley 45. That's like a cannon ball. It would have been like being hit by a train. No way he could have got up after to plug Paget-Bourke. And if Paget-Bourke had been shot first, there'd have been no chance in hell of him being able to level a howitzer like that Webley and get a shot off. Not on target.'

'Your forensic people never went into that, did they?'

'Happy to draw a line under two rotten apples, I reckon,' Bradley said. 'Close up two cases, as Jean said. And let some particularly gamey Parliamentary dogs lie. That doesn't prevent it, of course, looking very much as if a third person was involved.'

'Or maybe two or three,' he added.

Time for another swig, Ethan decided.

'Where's Saunders now?' Bradley went on.

'Last I heard he was down near Guilford, enrolled as a mature student in some kind of Agricultural or Horticultural college. He wants to go into landscape gardening.'

Bradley nodded enigmatically.

'So what happened to the portrait?' Jean asked.

Safer ground here.

'I made him a present of it. Thought it might boost his self-confidence – which really needed doing.'

'That was generous of you,' Jean said. 'It was really good.'

For perhaps the first time that evening Ethan's response was spontaneous and unconsidered.

'You've seen it?' he said.

'Yes.'

'How? Where?'

'On my PC in the Antiques Roadshow.'

'Excuse me?'

'My apologies,' Bradley said swiftly. 'I should have made it clear when I introduced Jean that when it comes painting you and she have a lot in common.'

'Oh?'

'I work out of Savile Row on a miniscule team that investigates dubious scams in the art world,' Jean said. 'The rest of the force have written us off as the Antiques Roadshow.'

'Dubious art scams?'

'Yes. One furrow we plough down is liaising into Europe on tracing the whereabouts of paintings and sculptures looted by the Nazis during World War Two.'

'Is that still going on?'

'You'd be amazed how many works are still untraced. Very occasionally we're able to return something to the descendants of the original owner.'

'Still?'

'Yes. Even today. The second thing we do is monitor and investigate the authenticity of works that have floated through the market and ended up either in museums or public galleries or maybe in private collections.'

'Sextons, you mean?'

'Yes. Possible fakes. Again you might be surprised. A painting or drawing will have been hanging on open display for years, its provenance unquestioned. Then a curator, restorer or some such will suspect a discrepancy. The seventeenth-century sketch is on Victorian paper, the brown in this Renaissance Madonna is invading its neighbouring colours so it turns out to be bitumen and a nineteenth-century copy. There's a tell-tale give-away and we have to trace who did what to whom in the Sales rooms.'

Ethan now found himself getting hooked.

'How did a nice girl like you end up being involved in a dodgy old world like that?' he asked.

'Oh – I had a degree in Art History and ended up cataloguing and curating at the Courtauld. Prestigious but a bit boring. The case of a forged Magritte came across my desk and – long story short – I transferred to the Roadshow.'

'Well, all my copies were done as a student trying to pick up on the tricks and techniques of my betters. Most of them wouldn't have fooled the blind.'

Jean smiled.

'I don't think we're after you for that,' she said.

Charming. Move on.

'Who are you after, then?'

'Right now we've got our eyes on a dealer. He's been around for yonks, has brokered dozens of respectable, perfectly legal, transactions. Hundreds, probably. But looking at work we know to be bogus, we've detected an interesting pattern. Does the name Rupert Penrith mean anything to you?'

Ethan shook his head.

'He's got a gallery-cum-shop in the West End.'

'And all kinds of contacts overseas,' Bradley added. 'America, the Middle East. Where the money is.'

'What kind of a pattern?' Ethan asked.

'Well, in the previous histories of these undoubted

forgeries,' Jean said, 'his name keeps cropping up as the middle-man in their coming on the market.'

'Well, perhaps he was fooled too.'

'Exactly what he would say if we braced him,' Bradley said.

'You haven't?'

'No. You see, overtly he's committed no crime. The pattern is that he approaches an auction house with a painting by, er ... er – '

'Corot, say,' Jean said. 'He'll tell them he found this languishing in some client's bottom drawer and say he finds it "interesting". What do they think? They, with the glint of a few thousand sovs already at the back of their minds, submit the fake to some "expert", someone of the ilk of Anthony Blunt, let's say. So it's the auctioneer-expert combination that authenticates the provenance.'

'So strictly speaking, legally, Penrith hasn't done a thing wrong,' Bradley summed up with heavy irony. 'Nothing-to-do-with-me-Squire time.'

'What interests us,' Jean took up, 'is that for years the Penrith Galleries have offered clients a Cleaning and Restoring service.'

'So that would be,' Ethan inferred, 'as in "I've got a blank canvas. Can you restore an original Picasso on it for me?"'

'Exactly,' Bradley said.

'We know that for years Penrith has employed a man called Kenneth Marsh to provide his gallery with nuts and bolts services – cleaning, stretching, reframing, re-backing, restoring.'

'And who knows what else besides?'

'Exactly.'

This time it was Jean who had spoken.

'Kenneth Marsh, fifty years ago, was a highly gifted, very

promising art student. The Royal Academy, no less. But he didn't kick on. He exhibited a little afterward but like so many, he dropped out of sight. He presumably ended up as Penrith's dogsbody to keep body and soul together.'

'Which hasn't finally worked out too well,' Bradley said. 'Jean has intelligence he is now a very sick man.'

'So if he has been providing Penrith with the occasional fake,' Jean said, 'that particular source is now closed down.'

'So?'

'Well,' Jean went on, 'on the assumption that Penrith, if only for everyday legal reasons, needs to replace Marsh, it would be so nice, really suit us, to slip an undercover agent in there so, poetic justice, we can get some chapter and verse authentic goods on him.'

For the first time that evening, Ethan realised why he had been bidden to share a friendly drink with senior coppers from two different divisions of Her Majesty's Constabulary.

'So that's what tonight has been all about,' he said.

'What?' Bradley po-facedly asked.

'You scratch my back, I'll scratch yours.'

Not altogether unpleasantly, the DI smiled back at him.

'You've got it in one,' he said. 'I knew you would. Fancy another?'

2

THE MORNING WAS NONDESCRIPT, DULL UNDER its uniform cover of grey cloud. With no sun to take the edge off, the wind blew chill and, despite the heavy, bulky artist's satchel slung from his shoulder, Ethan Shaw made a point of walking briskly eastwards along Piccadilly. Dorset Street, he knew, was only minutes away from Green Park. Ah, there! It was one of the modestly distinguished side streets running down towards Pall Mall two or three blocks away to the south.

The Penrith Gallery was not hard to find and staring at the premises from across the street he realised he had passed by it on numerous previous occasions without really clocking it. It was one of various art dealers' premises scattered here within convenient spitting distance of Fortnum and Mason's. Singled out for special consideration, The Penrith Gallery looked somewhat Dickensian. Its frontage was narrow but the division of the angularly shaped bow window beside the recessed glass front door into smaller window-barred rectangles conveyed a hint of Old Curiosity Shop authority. Hmm. Curious indeed to restrict vision to the viewer when your core business was peddling pictures: playing hard to get, perhaps? Currently, foursquare on a display easel set within the window, just one picture offered itself for inspection. Pausing to allow a taxi to pass by, Ethan crossed Dorset Street to examine the painting more closely.

It was a still-life – Dutch or Flemish certainly – of various dead animals. Game. A partridge, a pheasant, a limp-looking hare. Every feather, every hair in painstakingly depicted place. Certainly seventeenth century, m'lud, and that was as much as he could say. Not without some merit. Along with a meticulous attention to detail, the artist, whoever he or she might have been, had caught the personal tragedy of each creature's death in the not quite extinguished life still faintly gleaming in their unseeing eyes. Hmm ... a curious choice for attracting passing trade in this animal welfare day and age. But again, perhaps Rupert Penrith was trying to use alienation to indicate fastidiousness. Other paintings seemed hung in the space behind the formal window display in the interior of the shop but with the light falling obliquely across the glass it was impossible to make out what they might be. Well, only one way to find out.

He pushed open the front door half expecting a bell to ring but feeling obscurely pleased that none did. It was his eyes he had to put to use. To the right as he entered the shallow room a young woman sat at a small and, as it were, suave antique desk set at right angles to the front doorway. Nothing occupied the space in front of the desk but hung on the dark hessian-covered wall directly opposite were two expensively framed seascapes. Oils.

The receptionist did not stoop to words but looked her enquiry up at him.

'Ethan Shaw to see Rupert Penrith,' he said. 'We talked yesterday on the phone.'

'Ah yes,' she said and glanced down at a species of desk

diary. 'I have to tell you that he's running a little late. He is in today but he's presently tied up with Lord Blesdale.'

She had definitely set out to impress him. Her initiative or the boss's orders? Since he wasn't impressed anyway, it didn't really matter. He looked at her more closely. Thin, in her early twenties, with her chalk-white complexion, bobbed hair a shade or two less than blonde, her high buttoned blouse and three hundred pound designer spectacles, she looked this very moment the height of prim and proper decorum but nonetheless managed to suggest that of an evening elsewhere, if you treated her unprimly and improperly, she would go like a train.

'If you'd be kind enough to bear with us for a moment' she said, and looked away.

He gazed about him. There was absolutely no sign of a chair in or on which he might sit. But again perhaps that was the idea. *Faux de mieux*, on carpet whose thickness might have been sufficient for sheep to graze on, he walked across the room to give closer inspection to the two hanging paintings.

A pair, in fact. Two seascapes of a kind. Ships at anchor in a harbour as seen from further out at sea. Dutch or Flemish once more and once again seventeenth century. Done in firm bold lines, realistically rather than impressionistically, the buildings crowding the moorings were, down to their colouring and the light upon them, virtually identical. Van de Velde, just possibly. Or whoever. There was no attribution alongside either work and certainly nothing so crude as a price tag. Too patrician an operation to mention filthy lucre, no doubt. And how to rate them anyway? They were all right if you liked that sort of thing. Not if you didn't. Whether either or both were the real McCoy or not, he hadn't a clue.

A babble of laughter and unintelligible conversation cut his cynicism short. Turning he saw two men entering the reception area through the interior door set in the wall opposite the front window. One was of average height, the other, leading the way, a good half a head taller. Ethan recognised this giant immediately.

Yes, of course! Gorgeous Gus, aka Lord Blesdale. From the red top press, from television news, he could place him now. Saddled by his parents with the family tree name of Augustus, Blesdale had provided copy for gleeful editors on many a slow day for hard intelligence in the news-room: a rancidly scandalous divorce; untold speeding tickets as he indulged his adolescent petrol-head predilection for luxury sports cars; a conviction and near sentencing for killing (eventually) a stag with a cross-bow. Since succeeding to his title prematurely, Blesdale had playboyed it up as only a rich, well-connected thug might dare. Well over six feet tall, he had the wide shoulders of a man who in the course of collecting his B.A. (Bullingdon Arsehole) had probably rowed bow for his college. Even now, with middle-age well upon him, those shoulders threatened to burst the tailored confinement of the clearly expensive Irish tweed suit he chose to wear in town. He was Vikingesque. Red-gold hair squirmed and swirled across his skull and, while he was no oil painting, the Van Dyck beard he affected did serve to soften the long slab of an arrogant sixth-former's face inbreeding had bequeathed him. He had pointedly blanked Ethan completely as not worthy of consideration. The shorter man, however, clearly Penrith, had caught his eye and nodded his acknowledgement as he escorted Blesdale to the street door.

'You'll definitely make one at the Jockey Club bun fight, then?' he said.

'Wouldn't miss it for the world,' Blesdale heartily shot back. A bully's voice.

'Splendid. Until then, then.'

They had shaken hands and parted. Penrith closed the door on the pillar of garish tweed and turned back into the outer room.

'Every apology for keeping you waiting,' he said to Ethan. 'When nobility descends from out of the blue, one must, it seems, oblige. Here. We can talk in here.'

He held open the interior door and, as Ethan sidled himself and his awkward satchel past him, spoke over his shoulder.

'Emily, if you fancy an early lunch today, feel free to take yourself off as of now.'

Ethan found himself entering an office whose carpet was an inch or so less plush than the one he'd left behind but whose overall effect was nothing but agreeable. This could have been the study of a relaxed university academic. A bigger version of Emily's desk outside dominated it to the right and behind it and its comfortable looking leather chair, a row of certainly custom-tailored shelves were stacked with dozens of books that somehow managed to suggest they had been read. Opposite the desk was an enormous and too big for the room reproduction of Vermeer's 'View of Delft'. A big window set into the building's rear wall let in plenty of natural light. Penrith had made for his desk chair.

'Not the original, alas,' he said with a nod to the Vermeer as he sat. 'Please.'

Ethan sat in the room's only other chair, a Georgian-seeming carver set in front of the desk. He uses that line with every new customer, he thought as he adjusted the satchel. He looked at Penrith.

With Blesdale departed, Rupert Penrith looked bigger. But

the best single word to describe him had to be plump. Plump and sleek. He only just escaped being fat – possibly largely on account of the exquisitely tailored mid-grey double-breasted suit he wore. The cheeks of his clean-shaven round face were decidedly plump, however pink and healthy they might seem; and there was something plumply sleek about his small, neat hands. They seemed almost to flash. That was it! The nails. It probably wasn't actual varnish but Penrith's finger nails had a gleam that only a professionally applied manicure could have delivered. Well preserved, the man must be – what? – in his late fifties. He still had a full head of hair. Dressed back *en brosse*, steel grey, it ran straight over his skull to the nape of his neck where, artfully thickened, it curved inward and up to suggest he might be wearing a helmet.

'Thank you for coming in to see me,' he now said. 'And thank you as well for shooting through those examples of your work. As best I could on screen I looked at them with great interest and was no little impressed.'

He gestured with his plump left hand towards the satchel.

'Is that the landscape I mentioned on the phone?' he said.

'Yes.'

'May I see?'

'Yes, of course.'

As Penrith stood and came out from behind the desk Ethan worked the bubble-wrapped canvas out from the satchel and handed it up to him.

'Thank you.'

Penrith took the watercolour over to the window and, angling it forwards and backwards, silently examined it.

'Very nice,' he said. 'Very achieved. I like the way you've bounced the perspective to and fro.'

'Thank you. That's was sort of the idea.'

'Where's it of?'

'A view near Box Hill. If it ever came to labeling it for a catalogue you could call it "Landscape near Box Hill".'

'In the grand tradition, yes?'

Where you might have expected a baritone, Penrith had a light, rather pleasantly high-pitched speaking voice. He turned back towards the desk and laid the canvas down upon it.

'Well I'm afraid I don't have much in the way of good news for you,' he said. 'To begin with, apart from the occasional word to an acquaintance, I don't act as an agent for any artist. Not in the manner of an actor's or writer's agent, say. Further, I seldom handle or get involved with paintings later than the Pre-Raphaelites.'

'Ah ... well. I thought I'd ask the question ... '

'I'm glad you did. I do occasionally come up to date and deal with the living. I like your landscape a lot. I'd be happy to put it on view here.'

'Really?'

'Yes, really. Since you're unknown – not a name – I couldn't peg it at more than ... well, four hundred. How does that strike you?'

'Four hundred! Terrific!'

'It needs framing, of course, but we can do that for you. That'll set you back eighty pounds.'

'Eighty!'

'We can defer that until there's a sale. And, tell you what, if there isn't, I'll make you a present of the framing.'

'Well ... '

'I'm not risking much. I'm confident that a picture of that quality and with that subject matter and at that price will catch the eye of several of my semi-regulars. I wouldn't mind having it *chez moi*.'

'Well, in that case – '

'Ah. Let me cut you off right there. I made it an iron-clad rule years ago not to let business stub its toe on my personal pleasures. Otherwise I'd have been bankrupt as a young man.'

'Yes. I understand. Don't mistake me. I'm overjoyed to hear you say that you'll handle it. I won't disguise the fact – I'm sure it's obvious – that right now I'm nothing short of well and truly skint.'

Penrith had eyes that, grey rather than blue, contrived to match his sleeked back hair. They seemed now, Ethan became aware, to be regarding him unduly sharply.

'The other thing in your portfolio that caught my attention,' Penrith said, 'is that venture you've taken into the Picturesque. That view of the Thames Barrier at night.'

'Ah yes. My Moonlight Sonata.'

'Light years away from the freshness of your Box Hill watercolour. What accounts for such a shift in styles?'

'Probably little more than that I happen to live within walking distance of the Barrier.'

'But you might have painted it at blaze of noon.'

'Well, I also live close to the National Maritime Museum. When I'm particularly uninspired I pop in there now and then to cleanse my palate, so to speak. They've got a picture in there of the former Naval College – same building really – seen by moonlight.'

'I faintly remember it.'

'Yes. Very John Martin. I saw it again not very long ago and had this nice little earner brainwave. The Thames has changed so much since the docks collapsed I thought I might revisit some of its most prominent landmarks and record them as they now are, six or eight maybe, in the Picturesque manner.'

'As many as that?'

'Yes. Come up with a series – the Water Barrier, Tower Bridge, Battersea Power Station, Chelsea Bridge, whatever. Then, with any luck, sell the whole bunch to a Thameside council or perhaps an institution or company based on the river – IBM, say.'

'Hmm. Not a bad idea at that. Is this the first?'

'And so far the only. I thought I'd gradually work my way upstream.'

'But it's such a change of pace. Wasn't that difficult for you?'

'Not really, to be honest, no. I whipped off a Beacham of the Pether on my smart phone when the coast was clear and took it home and copied it. I mean as a student I'd copied the odd Van Gogh or Bonnard just to see what made them tick. This was a doddle after those.'

'Oh?'

The grey eyes were very sharp and narrow now.

'Yes, as we both know,' Ethan Shaw said as casually as he could manage, 'with someone like the Pethers or John Martin the dark values, the absolute black, are so prevalent you're off to a flying start. Though I say it myself, with the light behind it, my trial run copy might have passed off for the original.'

Somewhat less than naturally, Rupert Penrith coughed.

'Forgive my impertinence,' he said, 'but am I correct in believing from what you've told me that you're a bit hard pressed for cash just at the moment?'

'And the rest, yeah.'

'And would you have an objection to grubbing away – just briefly – at the bottom of the pyramid?'

'Meaning what? No, not if there were a pay check at the end of it.'

'It would most likely be cash in hand.'

'Even better.'

'You see we do offer cleaning and restoring services as a bread and butter sideline. Any experience along those lines?'

'Cleaning, yes. A smidgin. A woman from the Courtauld came down to Goldsmiths and talked about her work. A sort of crash course.'

'So it was hands on?'

'Well, I made it so. Afterwards I picked up a couple of junk paintings from a very junk shop and cleaned them up and sold them on.'

'Well, we've been cleaning seriously well worth pictures for years. I've had this quite brilliant, er, craftsman working for me for ages. Kenneth. Thing is, though, that now he's a very sick man. A couple of months ago the two of us had to face the grim facts and, very regretfully on my side, we parted company.'

'Well, yes ... but I wouldn't fancy being let loose on a Leonardo.'

'Oh, we're not talking up to that level. Look – how would it be if I got the two of you together and Kenneth marked your card for you a bit?'

'And checked me out at the same time?'

'Well. Yes. That too. But I'm pretty sure the pair of you would be singing off the same song-sheet in no time at all.'

'What have I got to lose?'

'Excellent. I'll give Kenneth a call, send your portfolio down to him so he'll know that he's not being stuck with a complete novice, and we can take it from there.'

Moving back into his chair Rupert Penrith scribbled a note into his thick desk diary. It seemed to Ethan that the dealer was looking even more sleek and plump than he had appeared on first sight.

3

THE GOGGLES KENNETH MARSH HAD LOANED him broke down the ground of the painting before him into a grainy canvas inter-weave. Ethan Shaw leaned forward toward the easel with his fiercest concentration. He worked the spirit-soaked cotton bud in his right hand gingerly across the thick, craquelured varnish. It wasn't so easy. You had to achieve the delicate precision required without tightening up so tensely you became stiffly awkward. Nevertheless it was working out. The hideous yellowed varnish was dissolving away thus causing its own superficial network of cracks to disappear as he wiped each treated finger-nail's width of the surface clean.

'That's it!' Marsh said from over his shoulder, 'it's coming along nicely. By George he's got it! I think he's got it! Those cotton-buds are worth their weight in gold. I've gone through shed-loads over the past twenty years – Poundsavers must rate me their favourite customer. But they give you so much more accuracy when push is in danger of coming to shove than does loose cotton wool. Even on a brush. You see. That's all there is to it. Just keep calm and carry on.'

The oil on the easel – in the event a confection of wild flowers crammed pell-mell into a luridly purple vase – might have been some Victorian Sunday painter's grotesquely ham-fisted bid for immortality.

'The truth is,' Ethan said, 'that this thing is so vile it would be doing it a kindness to leave it covered over with all its surface muck and veiled from clear sight.'

'Not so much garish as gaudy,' Marsh replied. 'The artist must have been seriously colour blind.'

'It must once have cost pounds,' Ethan observed. 'Two or even three.'

'Including the frame.'

The house had been easy to find. Set in Chiswick closer to the river than might have been expected, it had turned out to be detached and surprisingly large. Edwardian probably. He had walked up the path to a neat, flower-bedded front garden and knocked firmly on a door that had chosen to present no bell to the world but instead a good, old-fashioned wrought-brass knocker. When, without any preceding noise from within, the door had suddenly opened, he had received a still larger surprise – the man confronting him was instantly identifiable as being at Death's door too.

He stood about five foot six and as such would once not have appeared unduly remarkable in a crowd. Not so now. Wasting him, disease had rendered him dwarfish. The neck extending up from his open collar seemed to have no connection with his blue American work shirt. The collar seemed two sizes too large for the scrawny collection of tendons and muscles outlined beneath the jaundiced, clutching skin. Equally the faded brown sports jacket seemed liable at any moment to slip from shoulders long since grown too sloping and puny to come near filling it adequately. But above all it was the shaking that indicated the physical deterioration of this human being. From the instant he had opened the door, Marsh's head – it had to be him – had been bobbing forward and back like a malignly conceived child's toy. It seemed unlikely the thin remnant of a neck would continue to hold it aloft much longer. Round, small, the face would once have appeared neat and alert. But now its features had been pinched to the gaunt and beyond. The eyes behind the inevitably too large spectacles were sunken and colourless. The glasses perched precariously on a nose sharpened pointedly towards the only destination left open to the life it fronted.

'Ethan Shaw?' Marsh said in a voice contriving to be both thin and husky at the same time.'

'Indeed,' Ethan said, 'and you, of course, must be Kenneth Marsh.'

Instinctively he had stretched forward his arm for the handshake. And instantly regretted it. The hand rising to meet his had quaked out forward, up, down, left, right like a dowser's rod and, when he clasped it, conveyed no sense of possessing any weight. His own hand had shrunk from crushing the thin, frail obscene-seeming bones it encircled.

'Yes,' Marsh said, 'so pleased to meet you. Prince Rupert told me all about you on the phone. He even e-mailed some of your work along to me.'

Still mopping and mowing he had sidled awkwardly backwards.

'This way.'

Shuffling rather than walking, Marsh led the way towards the back of his house down a broad, parquet-floored corridor. To the left, a handsome wooden staircase right-angled its way upstairs. Marsh had ignored a first interior door to his right but shakily opened a second.

'In here,' he said.

His slippers scraping, he had entered what was clearly the rear of the house's main room. Ethan followed him through the doorway and then stopped short in further surprise. The large room did indeed complete the original house but, its French windows already ajar, it backed onto the extension of a wide and deep conservatory over-arching up towards the second storey.

'This is my drawing room,' Marsh said with the faintest of smiles, 'and on behind it, of course, my painting room.'

'It's splendid,' Ethan said spontaneously, glad to have something cheerful and positive to come out with. 'What a perfect set-up.'

'The back of the house is north-facing,' Marsh said. 'So – shall we go through?'

Slowly, so as not to outpace his shuffling host, Ethan crossed the room. Apart from a handsome 1930s-ish padded sofa, a complementary armchair and a huge television screen angled across the far corner, the room was barren of furniture. It scarcely looked lived in. There was an excellent reproduction of Piero's Pregnant Madonna on one wall and another of Raphael's Galatea on another but not a single sign of a family photograph or snapshot.

Marsh had halted by the side of the French windows.

'After you,' he murmured.

Ethan stepped down to the tiled floor of the conservatory. It was as large as the rear room but also markedly empty. To the far right a long trestle table stood stained all over with dried up splashes of faded colour but completely devoid of pots, brushes, cleaned palettes or tools of any description. In the centre of the conservatory, an easel was placed opposite a tall wooden stool and a be-cushioned canvas director's chair. On the easel in a clunky frame rested a painting which, from the angle he was looking at it, seemed to Ethan to be no more than so much petrol spread across a puddle. Alongside this stool, he now saw, was a thin table on which various glass bottles and jam jars with brushes had already been placed. Despite the strong visual sense of fresh air crowding the conservatory's windows from outside, the atmosphere within was deathly still and laden with the pungent aroma of turpentine and dammar varnish.

'Rupert asked me to check you out on basic cleaning,' Marsh said, 'so I've fished out something eminently in need of a wash and brush-up while being no less eminently expendable.'

'Probably just as well,' Ethan said as he moved to the stool.

'Do you live here by yourself?' he risked.

'Since my wife died four years ago,' Marsh shakily replied. 'I have a carer who comes and kick-starts my mornings, gets me up and helps me shower. But once that's done I can manage quite well for myself, I find. It's an Ocado and ready-meal sort of life these days.'

'You've no other family?'

'One daughter, long since estranged – she took her mother's side,' Marsh said again without audible resentment. 'Shall we give it a go? It's all common-sense really. Here, put these goggles on.'

Moving to the stool Ethan had tried to recall the very little he genuinely knew about cleaning canvases but took immediate heart from the pig's breakfast of a painting now facing him. The process was long overdue. Neglect over long years had seen to it that the initially applied over-thick layer of varnish had hardened, yellowed and grown crazed the length and breadth of the modestly sized canvas. Further, it was now evidently discernible, the main image it obscured was scarcely worth the rescuing. Marsh had chosen well. To blunder here would not cost Mankind a masterpiece. And in the top right corner, in the still life's shadowy background was a virtually dead area where he might do little in the way of harm ...

Conscious of Marsh's quavering presence behind him, he had gritted his teeth and started to apply himself. Occasionally, always positively, Marsh gave him a tip.

For the best part of an hour he soldiered on. His dabbing became more fluent. He moved from blue to yellow petals with more confidence and with an instinctive recourse to a fresh brush or cotton-bud. There was still a long way to go.

'There,' a voice said. 'I think we might call a halt there.'

Kenneth Marsh's voice. High and wheezy. He'd forgotten that he was there!

'You're clearly finding it no problem' Marsh said. 'And the picture's not worth saving for itself. I'll bin it tomorrow.'

Pleased at this verdict, Ethan sat further back on the stool. His back he discovered was aching.

'No great loss,' he said. 'But I could do with a break.'

'Dear me! Marsh exclaimed. 'What must you think of us? I haven't so much as offered you a cup of tea!'

'No, really.'

'I'd offer you one now – '

'No – '

' – and a sandwich or something. But to tell you the truth, I'm feeling a little bit jaded this morning. If you'll forgive – '

'Well, can I do you a cup of tea? Just point – '

'No, no, no. I'll have a little lie down. I'll be as right as rain in half an hour. Perhaps if you can bear dragging out here again tomorrow we could have a go at your "A" levels.'

'"A" levels?'
'Restoring.'

Hammersmith to Chiswick was no drag at all. The next morning found Ethan reaching for the brass knocker on the dot of the appointed hour. He had less time to wait on this occasion. Kenneth Marsh stood before him seemingly wearing the same shirt, the same jacket and, shaking and bobbing, still very much the same man in the full grip of Parkinson's.

'Well done,' he said. 'It costs nothing to be punctual.'

As he entered the conservatory this time Ethan found himself confronted by what at first glance seemed a far better painting than the previous day's Victorian trash. Frameless, it was a head and shoulders portrait of a fairly young, pleasantly featured man draped in vaguely Roman fashion in a free-flowing robe of russet brown silk. The portrait had suffered a patently visible graze to the dark background beyond the subject's three-quarter profiled pose.

'Who would you say that's by?' Marsh asked.

'Not sure, actually,' Ethan honestly replied. 'A sight better than yesterday's. Seventeenth century, I'd say. Probably English.'

'Yes ... ?'

'Too homely, not air-brushed up enough to be by Van Dyck or even Brown. Not glossy enough ... '

'No ... ?

'So you go on to Lely or even Kneller ... but it doesn't quite have the bravura they would have given a sitter. Er ... '

'How about Mary Beale?'

'Oh, of course! She was in Lely's studio, wasn't she?'

'She was indeed. One of his assistants. When he died she was asked to finish off some of his uncompleted stuff.'

'I'd completely forgotten her.'

'Shame on you. Later on she set herself up in her own right. She was England's first ever female, self-supporting professional artist. The "paintress" she became known as. That's her husband there, Charles. He had the sense to recognise a good thing when he saw it and turned himself into her manager and agent as we would say. Now, how are you going to make good that graze?'

'I'm not entirely sure.'

'First you're going to single out an 00 sable brush. Here, I've done it for you. Then you're going to mix a black exactly the shade making up the background there. We can do that in terms of colour. Of course with what I've got here we can't manage an exact chemical match – there's about three hundred and fifty years between the two paint stocks and a spectroscope can tell the difference.'

'Well, should we do it at all, then? The painting must be worth a bob or two, even as it stands.'

'Not really,' Marsh said. 'I was exaggerating a bit back there. It's not exactly a Mary Beale.'

Ethan swivelled on his stool to see the emaciated and wobbling face of his mentor grinning at him from underneath the over-the-top spectacles.

'It's a Kenneth Marsh,' Kenneth Marsh said.

'You mean – '

'One of two actually – two that are virtually identical.'

'The original and – '

'No. Both mine. Once upon a time Prince Rupert asked me to knock one out because he had a client – a punter, really – in the market for a Beale. So, since he was going to make it worth my while, I obliged. I did the one to see if I could – this one – and then did it again with old-style pigments I ground and mixed myself. That took some trial and error, I may say.'

'Where's that one, then?'

'Oh, it's where it's been happily hanging for decades – in said punter's household somewhere up North. He's a happy bunny, I dare say.'

'Why are you telling me this?'

'I damaged this one intentionally for your benefit. Let's see what you make of it.'

'Well ... I don't want just to paint over it. On anything like a close examination my stroke will never match the orig – yours.'

'Quite right. Well done. The answer is to stipple it.'

'Ah. Obvious when someone tells you.'

For the very best part of a further hour of intense concentration, using the superfine sable brush and employing the magnifying goggles to full advantage Ethan practised what Marsh had preached, stabbing fine beads of paint home upon the damaged surface.

'Don't overcharge the brush,' Marsh enjoined, 'and don't make the paint too moist. You're applying almost a bubble. As the paint dries each bead will flatten and spread and mingle with its neighbours. Not pointillism, you see, you're seeking to blur. Tomorrow morning you'll have a dull, uniform, continuous surface. Invisible mending, we used to call it.'

'Right now it sticks out like a sore thumb.'

'Patience is a virtue. Wait for what the morrow will bring.'

'So you forg – copied this.' Ethan felt their new acquaintanceship could stand.

'Well, yes and no.'

'Meaning?'

'Well, him being her husband and agent, Mary Beale always had him around. She polished off six or seven portraits of him. Presumably as a way of keeping her hand in between commissions. When times were bad she actually painted him on sacking. What I did was to take a look at most of her studies and then work a teeny-weeny variation on them.'

'Why?'

'To muddy the waters a little. She's not exactly in the top drawer, so the discovery of an addition to her oeuvre was never likely to attract the world's top authorities and have them label it as a proven forgery, as you nearly called it. And additionally she had two sons, trained by her who were also capable artists and, not so surprisingly, painted exactly in her style. So, critical assessment coming to shove, who could say for sure that one of them hadn't produced this? In the event of a worst case scenario arising regarding this version, its provenance could almost certainly be lost in the shuffle. What I did was frame Charlie boy there fractionally looser than was her custom and twist his pose round half a turn from her usual full- face handling.'

'You've done that very well. Squint and the portrait is almost pure profile. Relax your gaze and you seem to see nearly the whole face.'

'Thank you. I did a good job on the further cheek. In real life you wouldn't see that much.'

'Why, though? Let me ask you again.'

'Why did I take to augmenting other artists' outputs?'

'Well, that too. But mainly why are you being so open about all this to me?'

Marsh audibly sighed.

'I'll tell you that in a moment,' he said, 'after I've shown you something. You've nearly done that now. Just finish off that last corner and I'll be right back.'

Not breaking his dot and carry one rhythm Ethan heard Marsh rise creakingly to his feet and shuffle back into the house proper. He had completed his last stitch, as it almost seemed, when a clattering of wood behind his back had him turning around on his stool. Making a flapping meal of it, Marsh was toting two rather large unframed canvases into the conservatory-studio.

'Take a look at these,' he said. With difficulty, breathing hard, he placed the two paintings face outward against the base of the house's rear wall. As he had been invited, Ethan got up from his stool and crossed the conservatory to look at them.

Large as the canvases were, they were both crowded by what they depicted. Both were outdoors scenes – one a river crammed with gaily bedecked launches, rowing boats, canoes and punts, the other a view of a wide sea-side promenade alive with 'Kiss-me-quick' holidaymakers streaming towards a pier that thrust diagonally through the middle distance towards a more grey than blue ocean.

Marsh let him take his time.

'What do you think?' he said at last.

'Well ... they're certainly competent. The paint's very well applied – the way the colours are juxtaposed, staggered, works wonders for the perspective. The figures are quite well realised ... '

'But ... ?'

'Once again I don't recognise the artist. The river and the costumes obviously make you think of Spenser but they're not hallucinatory enough for him ... Young Spenser? I don't think so ... there's the faintest hint of Lowry but the draughtsmanship is too exact for it to be him ... not quite Ravilious either.'

'Do you like them?'

'Not enough. Competent but they don't sing. They're inert, somehow, for all the movement implicit in the subject matter. They seem to be hanging fire.'

'Agreed. You're right,' Marsh said. 'I think "torpid" might be the word for them. They're mine by the way. I did them.'

'Well when I said – '

'No. Don't waste what little time I've got left by manufacturing an apology you don't for the moment sincerely intend. I wasn't trying to trap you. You have exactly the same opinion of them that I've long entertained myself.'

'Then why – '

'I showed them to you as a moral to point a tale. Look, you and I know two things for sure, don't we? We know precisely why Rupert Penrith sent you here to learn at my knee; and we know that I am not long for this world, don't we?'

'I ... suppose so.'

'As I mentioned, Prince Rupert shot some of your work along to me. It's good, very good. It's different to what I was doing when I was your age but it has the same brio and attack that I had in those days. You're too good to end up the same way that I have. You owe it to your talent to aim for something better.'

There was a curious expression on Marsh's ever twitching face, partly upbrading, partly defiant. It wasn't a moment to sit in judgment.

'How many?'

'Oh, not so many. Still out there, that is. About a score of sketches. As many again paintings.'

'Such as what?'

'Oh, a couple of Augustus Johns, a nice little Corot.'

'Really! And the paintings?'

'Nothing too grand or attention grabbing – a Vanessa Bell, a Claud Rodgers. Probably best you don't know others.'

'When did it start?'

'Ages ago. Not long after I left the Academy. Although I say it as shouldn't, I was a nifty draughtsman in those days. I needed a job to keep body and soul together so I ended up doing Penrith's running repairs. Quite legit. Then he clocked I was handy with a pencil. It all followed.'

'What on earth made you agree to get involved?'

'The money. What else? You'd say this house was a pretty good one, yes?

'I've been admiring it.'

'Built just before the First World War. Before the trenches. When builders could still get their hands on properly seasoned timber. It's worth a bomb now, though God knows who is going to cop it. It cost me a pretty penny when I picked it up, but I'd fallen in love with it, so I mortgaged myself up to the hilt and Penrith knew as much. So he baited his hook to the half converted, so to speak. It wasn't entirely the money. The cunning bastard sort of made out it was all a bit of a lark. And I fell for that. I got a distinct, bloody-minded satisfaction in knowing I'd put one over those toffee-nosed connoisseurs, so called, in the auction houses and little magazines who, truth be told, never knew shit from putty.'

Marsh's wheezing tones halted completely for a moment and, turning, Ethan was surprised to see the perpetual bobbing and weaving had also ceased as well. Clutching the arms of his director's chair with either hand, Marsh had become stock still and there was something of pride and dignity in his no longer quite so pinched face.

'I'll have you know,' he said, 'that in a world-famous gallery – not in this country – there's a side room dedicated to displaying nothing other than one of mine.'

'One of your what?'

The shakes took hold of Marsh again.

'Beyond saying "think Fauve" I won't tell you,' he said, 'and then you can spend your days trying to figure it out and track it down. I went to see it myself once. An odd feeling to see it in situ. Had a job holding my tongue. You wouldn't think it now, looking at me, but in those days Margot and I well and truly lived it up – holidays abroad, the Gritti, the Adalon, gourmet meals. I had a Lagonda, once, then a Sunbeam-Talbot. Lovely cars. Then, just before Allegra came along, I commissioned this conservatory.'

'So – back to the drawing board.'

'As you might say. The sketches were always the easier option. The paintings were much better money-earners but they took so long – all that securing old canvases and concocting pigments the old way. Not to mention the attention to detail at the easel hour after hour.'

'The sketches were quicker?'

'If you could get the paper, yes. Penrith came up with a very simple strategy. Think of an artist or engraver – Piranesi, say, Samuel Palmer – and consider their completed works. Then don't try to copy them or match them but dash off what could be taken as a preliminary sketch for one such. Preliminary but not identical – probably less happy in its overall lay-out.'

'What medium did you use?'

'Oh, the lot. As appropriate. Charcoal, bistre, pencil. Sometimes ink and a wash.'

'What on earth did you do about provenances?'

'Ah, good question. Penrith's department again. You're aware that forty years ago and even still today this sceptred isle of ours was pock-marked with belted earls at their wits end trying to take care of death duties and pay off the repair job to their several acres of ancient roof tiles.'

'Yes, of course. Stock figures of stage farce. Sell off the family silver time.'

'Or family old master. Penrith has been involved in finding buyers for umpteen not so negligible works. All on the quite up and up. Most of the time he's been a thoroughly honest broker usually doing a good job on the seller's behalf.'

'But ... '

'But once in a while he's been able to exploit his having the entry into all these not so stately homes. Once, I know for a fact, he smuggled one of my fearful symmetries, as I liked to call them, into Downton Abbey, let's say, and then "discovered" it on a later visit. Usually, though, he would do a deal with the aforementioned belted earl who, truth to tell, could be counted on as being no more pure as the driven as the next man.'

'When the next man is you.'

'Guilty, m'lud, as charged. All Sir Jasper basically needed – needs – to do is swear on a stack of Bibles that the interesting little sketch that might be by Stubbs has been in the family collection since great-great-uncle Henry acquired it generations ago. Of course in bringing the Stubbs to market, Penrith would never go beyond "school of" and "possibly by" in his attribution.'

'Nothing to do with me, guv.'

'Exactly.'

'But you kept knocking him out ... dodgy products.'

'In effect, yes. Quite early on I went to him and said I was finished with all this jiggery-pokery, but he said, "Oh yes, how are you going to go on living in the style to which you and your wife have become accustomed?" I didn't have much answer to that and I knew that I was already into it too deep for comfort if we seriously quarrelled. But I did try going straight for quite a while and concentrating on my own stuff.'

'But that didn't work out?'

'No. As I demonstrated. I'd take up my sketch book, sit at my easel, but every line I drew reminded me of Poussin or Rubens or Picasso, every colour I painted was from El Greco or Miro or Van Gogh. I had a thousand painters and their styles revolving around on top of each other in my head and no style of my own. I was ... utterly inhibited. I was like a musician trying to compose with a dozen radios all tuned to different channels blasting out in the same room.'

'That must have been horrible.'

'It was. I drifted back to my wicked pastiche ways.'

'When was the last time you crossed the line?'

'About two years ago. Just before this wretched ataxia got me well and truly in its grip, ho-ho, and started to shake the life out of me. In fact, it was doing a job on me even then. I told Prince Rupert I didn't think this swan-song effort was going to cut the mustard like the previous ones. But he said not to worry, he had in mind a direct sale to a private buyer who didn't know arse from elbow when it came to art.'

'So what happened to it?'

'No idea. But it was the last. As you have readily discerned I no longer have a snowball's chance in hell of accurately applying a brush to a canvas or a crayon to a pad. These days I can't paint as much as a barn door. My occupation's gone.'

'That must really hurt.'

'It's unbearable.'

There seemed to be nothing he could say to that. Ethan looked his sympathy toward Kenneth Marsh and found that once again the dying man had willled himself into a momentary immobility.

'You've got a spark,' Marsh said, 'talent.'

He began to shake again.

'That's why I've taken you through all this. I could carry on and show you how to repair an old canvas that's got a substantial hole punched through it – a stopping of flake white and gesso powder mix applied with a palette knife until flush and then imprinted with a bit of matchingly textured canvas, if you really want to know – but what I think I'd much better do instead is tell you to go straight back to Dorset Street and, without quite giving him a blow by blow account of our conversation, tell Penrith you've got no intention of becoming his hewer of wood and drawer of water or anything else.'

'Do you think you can make it to the nearest pub?' Ethan said. 'I'd like to buy you a drink.'

4

ETHAN SHAW DISASSOCIATING HIMSELF FROM THE Penrith Gallery was not exactly short and sweet but, thanks to a wholly unlooked for ameliorating circumstance, not as bruising an experience as he had expected. Saying nothing of what Kenneth Marsh had so surprisingly confessed to, he had based his decision to walk away entirely but reasonably on the grounds that he now perceived that working full-time as a restorer of other men's ailing paintings would leave him little or no time to pursue his own career as an original artist. Sitting behind his big desk in the academic-like inner office Penrith had made it quite clear that he considered this was a decision he had every right to sniff at. He had sucked in his plump pink cheeks and, pursing his no less plump red lips, looked down his wide, fleshy nose.

Nevertheless, clad in a navy blue clone alternative to his double-breasted grey suit, he had not violently exploded.

'I find this unfortunate,' he said. 'It inconveniences me. However this is a cloud that does have a silver lining.'

'Oh?'

'I've succeeded in selling your watercolour landscape.'

'Really? Who to?'

'To Khalid Nahkla.'

'Er ... '

'Yes, the name might well ring a bell. He's the Kuwaiti billionaire who owns Yellow Aster, the filly that did the One Thousand Guineas and Epsom Oaks double.'

'Oh, of course! As seen on TV.'

'He's been an acquaintance of mine for years – well we were at school together – but he's been a proper friend for a couple of years now, ever since we ran across each other at Lingfield. The Turf is an absolute passion with me too.'

'Right. The sport of kings. And sheiks.'

'He dropped in the other day to pick me up for a spot of lunch and fell for your picture at first glance. He said it was so totally English.'

'Well, there's no denying that.'

And not a Kenneth Marsh either.

'I managed to get him agree to six hundred pounds so I trust there's no objection in the circumstances to my setting the commission at twenty per cent.'

'Er ... no ... none at all. It is, after, all my first grown-up sell.'

'Indeed. And rather a prestigious one at that. We must try to get word around. All in all our brief encounter has borne worthwhile fruit for both of us. It may well be you're ordering your priorities as you should do. If you've any other landscapes on the stocks, I'd dare say I'd be interested.'

'It's a good thought.'

'So perhaps in view of the little local difficulty you've saddled me with, might I ask you to stay with the Gallery until I can make alternative arrangements? Say until the end of next month?'

'Yes. Fine. No problem.'

'Excellent. Thank you. I'll write you out your cheque right now.'

Buoyed up by the knowledge that two days previously he had paid into his bank account the largest cheque ever to come his way, but intimidated by the several thousand pounds worth of the carefully wrapped still-life he was carrying in his satchel, Ethan had splurged on a taxi. He was thus actually in advance of the appointed hour the third time he fetched up before Kenneth Marsh's front-door brass knocker. Before he reached up to grasp it he paused and took a deep breath. The painting he carried was no trial run exercise, unknown though the artist might be, it would be worth that small fortune to its current owner and after nearly four centuries of accumulated neglect was in dire need of not only tender but seriously professional loving care. It was a heavy responsibility for a novice. Penrith had his penny-wise pound-foolish nerve settling it on his shoulders. He drew in another breath. Well, he would have Marsh's quivering but calm advice to aid him. If it came to a sticking point he would under- rather than over-egg the pudding and let the not quite well enough alone.

He grasped the knocker resolutely and rapped at the door.

It did not open immediately to visit that funny doorstep feeling of expected surprise upon him. It did not open at all. He shifted his weight from foot to foot. To no magic avail. The door remained firmly shut in his face. Straining his ears, he could detect no slip-slop shuffling of carpet slippers.

Well, if Marsh were on the loo or merely upstairs it would take half a light year for him to get down that staircase. He knocked again longer and longer. Nothing. Hmm ... For all his obvious ailments Marsh had never indicated he was deaf. But perhaps ... On sudden impulse Ethan stepped off the porch and cut across the tiny front lawn, past the front windows of the house and on around its further corner. A side path of beaten clinker led him through to the back garden. He had a renewed sense that the garden was large for suburban London but what immediately pre-occupied him was the conservatory which he now stood alongside. A single glance told him it was deserted. In slightly ominous fact it appeared thoroughly lifeless. The easel was still in place but the tall, thin table that had been topped with brushes, benzene, methylated spirits, turpentine and rags was no longer beside it. The easel looked lonely but the French windows to the house proper were still wide open. Ethan turned the near corner of the conservatory and went to its own outer doors. They were locked firmly fast. It would be very easy to break the wide expanse of glass fronting him ... but he shouldn't do that. It would be pure over-reaction. Marsh this minute was probably standing in his open front doorway staring into vacancy. Hmm ...

He turned on his heel and went back up the side-path. As he turned into the front garden he at once detected movement. A woman was walking determinedly up the garden path. She halted abruptly when she saw him and the two of then stared hard at each other.

'Who are you?' she bawled out. 'What do you think you're doing?'

She certainly had her point. For a moment he did not say anything.

'I'm a colleague of Mr Marsh,' he came out with at last. 'I came to see him about a picture.'

He swung the satchel containing the still-life towards her as if it might be a passport or entry visa and so confirm his good faith. It seemed to cut no ice with her.

'We had an appointment for right now,' he went on. 'I

knocked at the door and waited but he didn't come – answer my knocking. I thought he might be in the studio round the back so I went to check. He's not there.'

The woman was middle-aged, foursquare and, hair bundled up in a scarf, was dressed like a housewife who has just popped out to the corner shop. She drew herself up a little straighter and taller but seemed to be possibly a little less suspicious. Her arm went into the large handbag she was carrying.

'He might have had another fall,' she said.

'Might I ask who you are?' Ethan asked.

'I'm his cleaner. I come in on Wednesdays and tidy the place up.'

Her hand emerged from the bag holding a key ring.

'I'd better go in and check,' she said.

She continued up the front path to the door and he moved across the lawn to stand behind her. At his own eye-level now, since she now stood on the porch step, she turned and, still wary, looked at him.

'You wait here,' she said.

She slipped a key into the Yale lock and, easily, the door swung open. She went on into the hall.

Ethan stood staring at the opening. That was all it was – an opening. He shifted the satchel from his shoulder and carefully laid it against the side wall of the porch. When he looked up it was still only an opening. And no sound. He held his breath and was aware of his stomach liquefying. With someone else doing the dirty work for you, it was impossible not to imagine the worst. He heard a breath that was not his own and there, suddenly, she was in the doorway again but this time looking at him differently.

She had changed. Her face was no longer stridently challenging but collapsed and chalk-white.

'I found this on the stairs,' she said in a voice that wasn't harsh and thrust a piece of paper at him. It was a sheet of plain white typing paper. A message had been printed across it in childishly irregular block capitals:

MRS P DON'T GO IN THE BEDROOM. CALL THE POLICE. THANK YOU FOR EVERYTHING YOU'VE DONE FOR ME.

The wavering script made the absence of a signature of no consequence.

'I don't have my reading glasses with me,' the evident Mrs P said. 'That's why I took a while.'

On top of everything, he realised, she was probably nine-tenths illiterate and needed confirmation.

'Have a sit down on the bottom of the stairs,' he said. 'I'll go and take a look.'

He pushed by her and into the hall. Even as the liquid in his guts congealed to ice he noticed incidentally, as if from far away, how handsomely the staircase – a light oak – had been carpentered. It debouched on to a landing of the same parquet as the hall. A fine oriental rug covered its centre, linking visually the two closed doors to the left. Not a hanging picture in sight. The bigger bedroom would be at the front of the house. He paused outside that one's door and then, steeling himself, turned the doorknob and pushed on through. It was as bad as he still had hoped it would not be. But thankfully muted. The curtains across the big front window were still closed and so the room was dim. The morning outside had been overcast and grey but nevertheless it still projected enough light against the curtains to silhouette the unmistakeable form of a corpse dangling motionless in the window bay. Drawn by some malign fascination Ethan moved towards the deceased in spite of himself.

Kenneth Marsh was no longer quivering. In death he had created a last awful image, the tongue protruding but purple rather than pink, just as the lips were blue and the cheeks livid. Unbelievably protruberant as well the open eyes, their whites skeins of burst veins, glared horribly in violent disbelief. Goya lived, Ethan thought and, as if rebuked by some deity for his impersonal levity, stumbled awkwardly as his foot caught on something on the floor. He looked down. Squashed on the carpet was the type of container pharmacists dispensed pills in and now, letting his eyes range more widely, he saw that beside the overturned tall, thin table beneath the hanging corpse lay a welter of similar plastic containers and cardboard boxes littering the carpet. All seemed empty.

There was nothing to do. There was positively nothing he could or should do. He went back to the door and out of the room. Mrs P stood up from the tread she was sitting on as he came down the stairs. She stared at him inquiringly with a cowed expression.

'Just as we feared,' he said. 'I'll call the police.'

He fished his mobile from his blouson's inner pocket.

'OK. Quick re-cap to finish off with,' Detective Inspector Ray Tanner said. Sitting with one leg over the other and at his elegant long-limbed ease on the classic 1930s-ish sofa in the drawing room which was no longer at Kenneth Marsh's disposal, he'd glanced at the notebook on his right thigh and then at Ethan Shaw in the big armchair opposite.

'You never touched anything up there?' he affirmed rather than asked.

'Nothing except the knob on the bedroom door. The outside knob.'

'Good lad,' Tanner said.

'I did tread on one of the pill boxes.'

Tanner shrugged dismissively. 'One down, twenty-seven to go,' he said. 'But you didn't know him well.'

'No. As I said, I came here to work on that painting over there with him.'

'To clean it up.'

'Yes. That was his profession. He worked for this West End dealer – '

'Penrith Gallery, Dorset Street.'

Tanner had glanced down at his pad again.

'Yes. There was talk of me taking over from him. But I'd just decided not go down that road.'

'When did you last see him before ... before today?'

'Ten days ago.'

'On the Monday then?'

'Yes.'

'Did he give you any indication at that time that he might be considering taking his own life?'

'Well ... yes.'

'What did he say?'

'Well, to begin with, there was his general, overall condition, he had full-bore Parkinson's. He shook like a leaf. All the time. Never stopped. Then he told me how despondent he'd become about having to give up his job. He was an artist you see. Had been. Now he couldn't control his movements so his lifetime occupation was gone. A man without an occupation doesn't have a life anymore. Does he?'

'Not unless he's a fuckwit,' Tanner said. He darted a doubly dark glance across the room.

'Excuse my Jamaican,' he said.

'I've heard the expression before,' Ethan said. 'Most frequently when I've used it myself.'

Across the room this time the two men exchanged easy smiles. Tanner closed the pad on his knee and leaning back into the sofa sighed. 'His neck wasn't broken,' he said. 'I've come across more than enough do-it-yourself jobs in my time and the neck never is. I wonder so many still go for that method. If you don't snap your neck – and you have to know your knots for that – it's going to take an awfully long time.'

'Perhaps they don't trust the pills. Think they'll wake up as vegetables.'

'A lot do, you know.'

'Perhaps it's a sense of tradition.'

'I doubt it. I remember one case in Kingston – well, never mind. This has to be all his own work, you know, no question. We've found a power drill bundled up in the bedding, the hook in the brickwork was shiny and new and there was powder all down the wall and over the skirting board. A thorough job. He clearly had a chemist's shop full of drugs in his belly when he stepped off into space. Maybe that sort of insulated him.'

'A pious hope, I'd think,' Ethan said. He had a flash vision of the gargoyle face again and silently prayed he'd be able to forget it.

DI Tanner looked at his watch.

'Thanks for your time,' he said. 'It's been a long day for you.'

'It has indeed.'

'Can I drop you somewhere?'

'Hammersmith?'

'Right on my way. No sooner said than done.'

5

'FANTASTIC!' DI JEAN STAFFORD ENTHUSED. 'A fantastic result! I never thought you'd get back to us with so much so soon.'

'I was very lucky,' Ethan replied across the table. 'If poor Kenneth Marsh hadn't known he was going to put an end to everything, I'm certain he would never have opened up to me like that.'

'It's a bitter-sweet result in any case,' Alec Bradley put in. 'When Marsh shuffled off his mortal he also deprived us of our star witness.'

'You know that Rupert Penrith was the true onlie begetter of all these scams,' Virginia Faulkner said. 'You can still go for him.'

'Not really,' Bradley said. 'He's never totally committed himself, has he, Jean?'

'Not that we know,' Jean said. 'It's always been "school of" and "studio of" when he's gone public on one of his so-called discoveries. We haven't got him red-handed.'

'At least he's stymied now,' Ginny said, 'lost his supply chain.'

It had been her idea the unlikely foursome should convene. When Bradley had phoned angling for another 'off-line debrief' in the Black Swan, she had abruptly gone onto the front foot.

'Why should you traipse across London to please his Royal Highness when there's a perfectly good pub just two minutes away from here around the corner? He coerced you – as good as blackmailed you – into this pantomime song and dance and you've rewarded the police with more than they could ever possibly have imagined. Bradley's indebted to you now.'

'He's a still water. I'm quite certain he knows exactly what happened there on Blackheath that night. We're lucky the police haven't thrown the book at us.'

'If they had done, you engineered our withdrawal so neatly the book would probably have missed.'

'It would have been hugely inconvenient for us. And expensive.'

'It's all blood under the bridge now. Call him back and invite him – and her – to dinner round The Thatched Cottage. Tell him we'll spring for it.'

So he had called Bradley back and, however frosty the initial reaction had been, here they now sat over their gastro-pub plates amid the hubbub of a heaving Friday night crowd. Ethan had entered the Thatched guardedly but relief had not been so hard to come by. After the introductions occasioned by Ginny's presence had been made, the two men had pushed their way through the bar to get a first round in.

'It was DI Tanner who tidied up Marsh's suicide, right?' he had said.

'Yes.'

'Good man, Ray. Excellent. Very analytic mind. Sees the wood and the trees at the same time. Very good at putting two and two together.'

'Seemed nice with it too.'

'He is.'

Bradley chose to give Ethan one of his more intentionally scrutable looks. 'Mind you,' he went on, 'in our line of work two plus two can sometimes work out as five.'

Ethan felt his stomach flutter.

'Oh?'

'That fracas a few months back in your neck of the woods. Those two filth who shot each other.'

'Yes, I remember.'

'Best thing that could have happened for all and sundry, if you catch my drift.'

' ... not really.'

'Well, let's pretend you have. I know for a fact a line's been drawn under that and it's gone away.'

'Really? That hasn't been in *The South London Press*.'

'I expect not. Happy endings don't sell newspapers, do they? Cheers.'

Ethan had returned to the table they had bagged lighter in heart than he had left it. Now – the surrounding clamour was more than proof enough to rule out any eavesdropping – he felt he was able to get something off his chest.

'In a sense,' he said, over his Cumberland sausage and mash, 'I'm glad Kenneth Marsh decided to do a runner.'

'Why so?' Jean asked.

'I wouldn't at all have liked standing up in the witness box and nailing him with his trade secrets.'

'Why not? He was a forger. A villain.'

'Yes. I would have done it, I suppose. But I reckon he was more sinned against than sinning. He'd been shunted on to the wrong track. He didn't know I was a temporary, acting, unpaid undercover agent, of course. What he came out with wasn't so much a confession as his confessional.'

'You think he had a guilty conscience?' Jean said.

'A little bit. As I've told you he was also proud of what he'd got away with. Mainly, though, he was trying to mark my card. I think he liked me. He said he liked my work. He knew he'd sold himself very short with his shenanigans and taking me at face value was trying to warn me not to follow in his footsteps. I have to give him a lot of points for that.'

There was a collective silence.

'It's all a load of bollocks really, isn't it?' Ginny said.

'What is?' Bradley said, 'your steak and kidney?'

'No, it's very nice actually. I meant this huge genuine or fake brouhaha.'

'How do you mean?'

'Well, it's all about images, isn't it? Van Gogh's "Sunflowers" say. OK, Van Gogh created them out of nothing so he gets full marks for creativity, imagination and inspiration. For originality – '

'And his technique,' Ethan interrupted.

'Yes. But if you set out to copy him – as you could – we'd end up with two identical images, one original, one if you like, a fake.'

'Virtually identical.'

'OK. But indistinguishable at a distance of six feet. Hang either one in a house or gallery and it will generate the same pleasure.'

'Probably.'

'Certainly. Hang them side by side, though, and the way it goes these days the one on the left is worth fifty million quid and the one on the right will set you back one and fourpence ha'penny. All right the one on the right may be interesting in itself purely because it is a forgery. But the one on the left is no longer a painting.'

'What is it then?'

'Oh – an internationally acknowledged icon. A hallmark of western European aesthetic sensibility or whatever other pseuds' claptrap those with a vested interest in Fine Art, PR and finance spout on about it.'

'The image is always going to remain Van Gogh's masterpiece,' Jean said.

'Yes. His intellectual copyright, as we now have to say. Give him every credit. But that still doesn't mean a copy, a decent photograph even, can't deliver the same effect. I mean, the world's masterpieces are scattered these days around the globe. You'd have to travel thousands of miles – tens of thousands – to eyeball a decent number of them. And when you got to New York or Florence or Saint Petersburg you'd find scads of gormless tourists parading by and getting between you and the walls they're displayed on. You're better off at home in an armchair with a first rate art book.'

'A photograph doesn't give you the whole picture,' Ethan said. 'The whole story that is. You don't see the brushwork.'

'Who says you're meant to?' Ginny snapped back. 'Oh, you're interested in the brushwork because you're a painter yourself and you want to learn this or that technique but when Rembrandt painted a shimmering white linen sleeve with a series of calculated stabs he intended the punters to see the overall effect. At a distance of ten paces, not through a magnifying glass. You know what Picasso said when they warned him people were forging his stuff left, right and centre? He told them to bring him these fakes and if he liked any of them he'd shove his name on the bottom! If he was good enough to fool the top auction houses, I'd be glad to have a Kenneth Marsh on my wall.'

'That's largely the point,' Bradley said. 'I've no doubt that some auctioneers are well aware of that. They're predisposed to want the forgery to be authentic. That's where a Rupert Penrith has a margin to operate in.'

'Yes, he's still potentially in play,' Jean said.

'Look, we've a very good idea now of what strokes he's pulled,' Ethan said. 'Can't you go through his records with a toothcomb and investigate any transaction he's had a hand in?'

'Well, at the cost of much blood, sweat and expense we might backtrack to individual works and prove them fakes,' Jean said. 'But I suspect there won't be a very clear paper trail in many cases. He'll have been too fly for that. He'll never have personally underwritten a fake provenance. It still won't be red-handed.'

'Perhaps he'll stick to the straight and narrow now,' Ginny said.

'I doubt it,' Ethan said at once, shaking his head, 'He's not the type. Can't resist temptation.'

'In which case ... ' Bradley began, 'how long before you kiss him goodbye?'

'What a horrible thought,' Ethan said. 'Another four weeks.'

'Well, any ways left for baiting his hook with?'

Ethan gave it some serious thought.

'Well,' he said eventually, 'when we were discussing my work the other day, he got seriously interested in a John Martinesque watercolour I showed him.'

'What's that when it's at home?'

'Essentially a landscape as seen by moonlight.'

'Pretty easy to forge,' Jean said.

'Well, there you are, then, Ethan.'

'Plus he did manage to sell one of my landscapes. I've got

another collecting dust back at mine that he made plain he'd like to help find a home for.'

They all looked at each other with a not so wild surmise.

'Look, they do coffee here,' Ginny said. 'But if you like, we could all go back to my place and have some there and a modest nightcap or two.'

Ethan and Virginia saw Bradley and Jean exchange identical looks.

'I think "thanks but no thanks",' Bradley said. 'I've got a sparrow-fart start in Brockley tomorrow.'

'No weekends for the Met,' Jean said. 'But tonight's been good. At the very least we've stopped the rot.'

'I'll settle up,' Ethan said as he started to rise.

'No – stay put,' Jean said. 'The labourer is worthy of his hire and the Antiques Roadshow is possessed of a tiny slush fund. It doesn't often get tapped, so let me take care of tonight. I can slip it by. Consider yourselves *bona fide* grasses.'

On the way back to her house just around the corner, Ginny gently nudged Ethan with her elbow and, looking up at him, asked a question.

'So are we to imagine Alec Bradley and Jean Stafford are an item?'

He had been wondering too.

'I genuinely don't know,' he said. 'She's a still water, too. They are of a certain age.'

'Just the age, I'd say,' Ginny said.

6

LATE ON THE AFTERNOON OF THE Sunday of the very next weekend Ethan had endured his Hammersmith to Charlton drag yet again and returned to the downer of the so-called, but in his case literally so, studio flat. In the five days he had been away only junk mail had piled up for him on the rickety table in the token vestibule. Without opening any envelopes he binned it the instant he was upstairs.

It had taken an effort to enter the one big room. The musty odour of dust and turps had given him pause in the doorway. He must find somewhere to paint closer to Ginny's. It was insane to keep this pit on. The cost in extra tooth-brushes would bankrupt him. And now he was stuck with spending the night here. Well, to his purpose: while there was still daylight he sifted through his thin stack of canvases to fetch out his reverse view of Box Hill. It wasn't the equal of the one Penrith had sold for him – in hindsight the emphasised projection of the south-facing escarpment was too contrived – but if you wanted countryside, this was countryside. And while his relationship with Penrith now obviously dangled by a thread, you had to think the fat cat inside the man might purr at being offered a second bite of the cherry. Any road up, the watercolour was a prelude to further contact.

Carefully he cut bubble-wrap from the fat industrial roll and wrapped the frameless painting round and cased it in his satchel alongside the anonymous Dutch still-life he remained stuck with. He glanced at his watch. God! Still so early! There was nothing worth sacrificing brain cells over on his stone-age box tonight. Inwardly sighing he settled down in the lone excuse for an armchair to renew acquaintance with his battered *Tom Jones*.

The next morning, after an initially too self-aware and sleepless night, he slept late. That was OK. It was better to miss out on the hassle of the peak rush hour and the aggro of manoeuvring his awkward but irreplaceable load in and out of the bloody-minded resentments of so many one-track minded commuters. By the time he had treated himself to a delayed croissant and coffee in the Piccadilly Pret-a-Manger there was plenty of elbow room to spare.

It was mid-morning, then, as crossing Dorset Street on a diagonal again he approached the Penrith Gallery only to find himself stopping on the pavement directly outside the premises in surprise. Something was wrong. The place was still shut. He'd been a fool to himself! Hadn't phoned in advance to let anyone know he was coming in. He'd had a wasted journey.

He tried to hope for the better. There was no light on inside the Gallery that he could make out and the high-tech metal shutters, that could be slid down over-night immediately behind the main run of windows and the largely all glass front door to protect originals or fakes, were still in place. It was in character for Penrith to be cavalier about his time-keeping but Little Emily wasn't earning her corn if she shirked her telephone-answering and sentry duties. Dammit! The satchel was weighing heavy and he had too much coffee inside him to make more killing time around the corner seem fun.

At a complete, frustrated loss, he struck down savagely at the old-fashioned handle fronting the door. It gave downward way at once and the door eased open an inch or two. Unlocked! No alarm bells were ringing as they should have been. The state-of-the-art Israeli locking system hadn't been activated. Listening intently, he prodded at the door. It arced easily backwards until nearly full ajar. A pedestrian's footsteps sounded on the pavement behind him. And then went on. But no sound from within. Nothing. The place was as silent as the grave.

He went into the small outer room and halted at once. To his left, close to the front window bay, someone lay on the floor. It was presumably a man since what his eyes first focused on were a pair of shining burgundy loafers and, yes, above them the grey trousers of a man's suit. Penrith, of course. Penrith's suit, anyway. He couldn't be entirely sure; lying at the furthest away point from where he stood, the head of the man was enclosed in a black cloth bag.

He was not thinking coherently now. He had slipped his clumsy to manage satchel to the floor. He was leaning close to the covered-over head. Get a grip, Shaw! This wasn't someone asleep, this was a corpse!

He didn't want to but he had to. Stealing himself, not breathing, he gingerly pinched the top corner ofr the bag between finger and thumb. Breathing harshly now, clenching his belly, he drew the cloth steadily up and away from the head. A terrible sight confronted him ... glared blazingly back at him. It was Penrith all right but what a transmuted Penrith! The always sleek hair was now a scarecrow's halo of grey-white tangles and tufts. The open eyes sightlessly broadcast bulging, outraged horror up at him. The rictus of a stretched taut, open mouth framed two rows of perfect teeth striving but failing to clench.

'My God! Not again!' was Ethan's first and selfish thought.

There was absolutely no point in searching for a pulse. All the same his benumbed gaze had automatically looked downwards for the wrist. Thus another shock assailed him. Penrith had collapsed or been arranged on his side in a semi-foetal position and in the area between his paunch and thighs the over-thick carpet was turned burnt-umber brown by a dried ooze of crusted blood. Where … ? My god! Oh, sweet Jesus!

A third hammer blow had driven him to the edge of disbelief. Wrist! What wrist? Penrith's left arm was intact but the blood which had soaked the carpet had drained out from the ragged stump that protruded from the right sleeve of the jacket. No right hand was in sight.

He had seen men on stretchers in Northern Ireland but nothing like this. So abrupt. So casual almost. For a second he thought he might faint and then as he tried to brace himself thought he would be sick.

Retching as his stomach slammed upwards involuntarily inside him, he leaned sideways and somehow avoided vomiting. To steady himself he staggered forwards to Emily's small desk and clutched its leading edge with both hands. He might yet be sick. He leaned forwards and closed his eyes.

Don't allow it to happen! Good! Feeling steadier now.

It was only when he opened his eyes that he saw what was on the desk. Something had glistened. Yes, it was the light reflecting from the polished fingernails on the hand hiding in plain sight dead centre of the blotter.

Severed, the hand seemed less plump and self-assured than it had been when attached to the living arm. Finger extended forwards it was lying flat and depleted, palm down.

No, he would not, could not, touch it.

Zonk! His throat had gagged in another unsought spasm and this time he was sure that he was going to throw up. But as he closed his eyes a second time, a monstrously high-pitched shrieking ascending into ululation, came piercingly home to his right ear. Opening his eyes to the sound, turning his head, he saw Emily standing in the front doorway staring down. Her hands were to her head as it snapped backwards and forwards. Hysteria. He knew what he had to do.

Himself again, he stepped forwards and slapped her fiercely on her upturned, slanted-back forearms. 'Snap out of it!' he shouted in to her pinched and bloodless face. 'Take hold! See what happens when you turn up late for work.'

7

AFTER HE HAD CALLED THE POLICE it all went on for a while. First a squad car had arrived and, looking grimly non-committal, two uniforms had noted a few preliminary details and talked a lot on their intercoms. Reminding him of Saturday afternoon at the Valley, a transit van had eventually turned up, bringing more uniforms. Two Detective Sergeants and enough yards of blue police tape to proclaim that the Penrith Gallery, and half the fronting Dorset Street beyond it, might well be deduced a crime scene. An unliveried saloon car now brought a DI Carter and a photographer.

While Carter put to him the same name, address, phone number questions he had already answered, the photographer happy in his possession of digital equipment flashed off exposure upon exposure as if there were no tomorrow.

For Penrith, of course, there no longer was. Eventually an ambulance came with paramedics carrying stretchers. The body was removed at last leaving behind in a manner that boggled the mind it's outline somehow chalked on the carpet by a spray can. Suddenly and surreally the Gallery's small front room seemed the backdrop for a *New Yorker* cartoon competition: supply your own caption. At last, seated in

Penrith's back office, Carter had taken him through the manner of his morning discovery and, struggling, he had tried to outline the nature of the business Penrith had transacted.

'If you want the names of client contacts, you'll have to ask the receptionist,' he said.

It was evening rather than afternoon when he got away. He hadn't been offered the chance of a quick bite all day. Just as well, he thought, I couldn't have stomached a thing but even so ...

Now he had to bear the brunt of the rush hour in full flood. He strap-hung back to Hammersmith. Then the quite long walk, as it now seemed, down King Street. Ginny had arrived home before him. As he let himself in by his own key, he felt unnaturally done in. When he stepped into the long, knocked-through living room he saw a type of concern on her face he had never witnessed there before.

'What happened?' she said tensely. 'Are you all right?'

'Well, something' he said. 'Over and done with now. Nothing for us to worry about. It's just that I need to come up through the decompression chamber for a moment. Sit down and I'll explain.'

'Well you sit down,' she said. 'I'll be back in a couple of shakes.'

He sat down. When she returned she was carrying two stonking great gin and tonics, lemon and cucumber included. He felt the coolness going straight to his stomach.

'Needed that,' he said. 'Now.'

As evenly and dispassionately as he could he took her through the course of his somewhat crowded day. Her eyes growing rounder and rounder, she listened without comment, her posture visibly tightening as he continued. When at length he had finished, his glass, he realised, was empty.

'We need to go out,' she said. 'Somewhere heaving.'

'Right,' he said. 'And I need comfort food. I've not had a thing all day.'

'The Bengal,' she said. 'Stick it to your ribcage food.'

'Perfect. Any more where those two came from?'

'Coming up in the next bucket.'

This time when she came back in her eyes had a sharp gleam in them.

'But one thing about all this sticks out as the proverbial spare prick at a wedding.'

'Oh? What's that?'

'Amputating a right hand. What does that put you in mind of?'

'What?'

'Think Arab, think Turk maybe, think Middle East.'

'Oh right. Thieves. Punishment fitting the crime. You think that's likely?'

'Why not? If there were Arabs about.'

'They're everywhere these days.'

'Look, when people are stressed, emotional they revert to type. Being out for revenge is a strong emotion. It brings out the traditional. Exact revenge the way your daddy did. Your grandfather. Think of the Mafia. If Penrith has crossed the IRA he'd have ended up knee-capped.'

'Well ... Do we need to book a table?'

'Not if we go right away. I'll just nip upstairs and change into something more comfortable.'

'I think I'll just touch base with Bradley.'

'Do you really need to do that now?'

'It will amuse me to be calling him for once.'

The receiving phone was allowed to ring only the once.

'Hello?'

'Alec? Alec Bradley?'

'Speaking'

'It's Ethan Shaw.'

'Ah, don't call me, I'll call you time. To what do I owe the honour?'

'Have you heard of today's goings on in Dover Street?'

'Dover Street?'

'The Penrith Gallery?'

'Ah. No. Not my patch. News takes its time filtering down to us in here in the provinces in Lewisham. What did go on?'

'Are you sitting down?'

'As it happens, yes.'

Keeping his account as brief and his voice as deadpan as possible Ethan brought Bradley up to speed on the morning's fun and games. When he had finished, he could hear Bradley remaining silent.

'Blimey O' Reilly!' Bradley said eventually. 'You really should change your name to the Angel of Death, shouldn't you?'

'How do you – '

'Every time you drop in on someone these days they end up Hovis.'

'Hovis?'

'Brown bread. Stiff as the wooden overcoat they're about to put on.'

'What do make of it?'

'Not sure yet.'

'Sort of puts DI Stafford out of business doesn't it? No forger, no con-man dealer.'

'No. She probably knows already but I'll have a word with her. Leave it with me. I'll make some calls off-line, see what I can dig up and get back to you.'

'I assume – I hope – all this puts me out of business too.'

'Seems like it might. Don't hold your breath, though. It might be a couple of days. I know for a fact that forensics is backed up all the way to Junction 27.'

'OK, I'll wait to hear.'

'Thanks for the call. Try to sleep tight.'

Click.

Bradley had predicted accurately. It did take two days.

During that interval while Virginia went to discuss hemline lengths for the next Spring collection, Ethan figuratively paced her too-quiet Hammersmith home. For two nights he had slept well, significantly, dreamlessly. It was when he woke and found himself being stared in the face by another day without purpose that his spirits quailed. Very occasionally, startling him, the house phone would ring. But that wouldn't be Bradley, and no, he didn't want to buy a case of South African Sauvignon Blanc at only £5.99 a bottle. He found himself beginning to regret not having used his smart phone to knock off a quick passport death mask of Penrith's straining final countenance and wondered how bloody-minded that made him. A professional craftsman, he had to hope. Nevertheless – better out than in – he settled down to attend to sketching the nightmare expression from memory. It wasn't truly therapy he knew, more the wish not to pass up the chance – bleep! Making him almost jump out of his skin this time, his phone had rung again and his charcoal had zig-zagged a miscue straight across the staring left eyeball. This time it was Bradley getting back.

'Are *you* sitting down?' he said.

'Sort of. Mentally.'

'Right. I've come up with quite a bit.'

'Oh?'

'First off – he didn't bleed to death. He died of heart failure.'

'Well, let's hope for his sake it was sooner rather than later.'

'He didn't lose that much blood it seems.'

'It looked like he had but the carpet there was – is – very thick. I couldn't tell how deeply the blood had sunk in.'

'Now here's the bit you won't like ... his hand wasn't hacked off – it was sawn off.'

'Jesus!'

'Exactly. The wrist-bone ended up totally corrugated and the flesh was all chewed up.'

'Ye Gods ... '

'You didn't touch him, did you?'

'No. Practice makes perfect.'

'Well done.'

'Only the black bag thing.'

'If you had, you'd have found him made of concrete. Forensics time the attack back to Friday evening. He'd been stretched out all through the weekend.'

'The gallery only opens up at weekends by special appointment. Too hoity-toity to make a habit of it.'

'Perhaps someone knew that?'

'Possibly.'

'What about that bag?'

'Maybe to make the assault more terrifying.'

'As it would.'

'Maybe to protect the attacker's identity. Chances are there was more than one. Although I reckon it might be a ski-mask job. There were a lot of bruises on his chest and his ribs, by the way.'

'Yuck. I didn't like him but all the same ... '

'Yes.'

'So look. If he died of heart failure, it could be they overdid it, that they didn't mean to kill him.'

'Given that his hand was sort of served up on the desk on display, I think that's quite likely.'

'So it will be a revenge attack. Payback time.'

'Might well have been.'

'I was talking to Ginny about it. She thought that. She said if the IRA had done it he would've been knee-capped but that amputating right hands was what Arabs do to thieves.'

'Well, Penrith was a thief and I can vouch for the fact that he had at least one Arab client.'

'Several actually. They're working through the list now. There's bugger all else they can be about right now. No DNA, no dabs, not even any CCTV.'

'I suppose whoever did it could be out of the country by now?'

'More than likely – a forty-eight hour plus flying start. Now. I had a word with Jean – DI Stafford – and it seems Penrith was skint. His private account was overdrawn and the business was only just in the black.'

'So he could have been needing a nice little earner?'

'Exactly so. And here's something we never told you. He didn't own the Penrith Gallery outright. He had a sleeping partner. One Leonard Walsh. I'd hazard a guess that in this instance the expression "sleeping partner" covers all eventualities.'

'A multitude of sins. Could it be that Walsh – '

'Jean doesn't think so. He only had a twenty per cent share in the business and there's no trace of him ever having taken an active role in it or having much in the way of Fine Art savvy. He used to be a solicitor apparently, but he copped a big inheritance way back and set himself up as a gentleman of leisure.'

'All the same.'

'Yes, all the same. To coin a phrase at this stage of the proceedings, "we're not ruling anything or anyone out".'

'Where's the body now?'

'In the morgue. There's an elder sister, so there'll be a funeral of some sort. Turns out he was an RC. But before all that, there'll have to be an inquest – the one featuring you as the star turn.'

'The second time I've had top billing. That's the bummer about being the Angel of Death – your days just aren't yours to call your own.'

8

AS MADE CLEAR AS CRYSTAL BY his considerate note to Mrs P, the manner in which Kenneth Marsh had departed this life was as open and shut a case as could be imagined. DI Tanner had made it evident to Ethan on their parting that the mills of British Justice were grinding slower than ever these days and the date of the necessary inquest would be distinctly later than sooner. No longer a student, unemployed, his windfall from the Box Hill landscape all but gone, he had expected the ensuing days and weeks to crawl by in a monotonous and worrying drag. He had been proved wrong. A flurry of foreground activity had sprung up seemingly out of nowhere to offer him more than enough diversion therapy. The chief distraction to preoccupy him had been the shifting of his studio base from East to West London.

It had happened largely by chance. The Wednesday after the weekend in which he had, for the third time, been first on the scene of an unnatural death, Ginny routinely away at her nine to five, he had sought to stiff-arm his growing cell-fever by ambling round to The Marquis of Anglesey for a pint of lunch. The tiny pub was crowded and loud. A long streak of milk at the bar was complaining tediously in to his mobile.

Oblivious of, or perhaps playing to, the gallery of their eavesdropping presence, this thin, blond, bespectacled young man of no more than twenty-five was whingeing his heart out to God alone knew who.

' ... be not before the end of the month. Hammersmith and Fulham have walked in and requisitioned the entire site. Apparently they can do this. They've given all the owners of the units eight months' notice, then the bulldozers will come in ... Yes, eight months. But Anton has already picked out some spot in Milton Keynes and is moving Ampersand up there lock, stock and barrel. So farewell the Argyle Estate ... Well, he's not moving me ... Milton Keynes isn't the sort of prospect I fancy now I've just settled in here. I've told him he can shove it ... No, quite a few others have shut up shop as well ... Others are hanging on. The council are offering newcomers a chance to come in at a peppercorn rent but who's going to sign up for a six months tenancy even if the rent is nominal ... '

The Argyle Estate! Just off the Goldhawk Road and only a five-minute stroll away. A nominal rent was worth five minutes.

Ethan polished off his ESB and headed north. Just before the Goldhawk Road he came to an alleyway such as you might expect to lead to a jobbing builder's backyard. He had often passed it without really taking it in. Now it sported an estate agent's board – the Commercial Division. Worth more exploration. He turned down the alleyway and, rather further than he had anticipated, found it opening out onto an asphalted area roughly the size of a football pitch. All alongside the touchlines, so to speak, rather dog-eared industrial units stood sullenly shoulder to shoulder. Some were faced with signage bearing company names and logos, some, wide doors flung open, showed people, employees presumably, performing desultory, inscrutable tasks. Some units stood closed and presumably empty. What was not to like about making further enquiries?

Half an hour later Ethan found himself sitting in a small inner office within the surprisingly extensive and business-like premises of an Acton estate agent. The enhanced scrabble-like letters on the Tobleronesque wooden batten in front of him on the desk told him that the young man sittting opposite was one Ralph Coates.

'It's a peppercorn rent because the lease is so short. Hammersmith and Fulham intend building high-rise council flats there as of the late autumn-winter.'

'Let's hope they've got the cladding sorted.'

'Indeed. What they're really after in the meantime is keeping the units occupied. They don't want them vandalised or, worse, infested by squatters and all the consequences that might bring.'

'If your need is only as short-term as you say it is, then, this could work out very nicely for you. You won't get so much space for your buck at this joke price anywhere else in London.'

'Can we take a look?'

In Ralph Coates' Astra they returned to the Argyle Industrial Trading Estate. Number 17 was indeed one of the already abandoned units. Its frontage consisted of two doors divided by a pillar of bricks. The one was a conventional single door, the other an extensive up and over door that stretched across to the neighbouring, and also unoccupied, 16. Coates opened the smaller, everyday door.

'After you,' he said.

Ethan found himself in a cheaply partitioned sub-area of the interior space that had clearly served as an office. A cheap desk, not so very different from Coates' own, remained empty and chairless close to the entrance. Behind the desk at some distance was a sink and butted up against it a chipboard run of counter that, with the addition of a microwave, might have been regarded as a kitchen.

'There's a loo at the far back,' Coates said.

'Right. Can we see the main bit?'

'Of course.'

Coates led the way through an interior door set into the partitioning and, following him, Ethan had the sense of entering a dark, musty, mouldering, cave. It was as black as Newgate's knocker.

'Let me find a switch,' Coates said.

There was a click. Overhead fluorescent tubes coughed, hesitated, stuttered again, and came on to stay. They dispensed a too-bright whitish light that allowed Ethan to see that he was standing in a space about the size of a squash court and that a screen of sorts had been stretched across the centre of the far wall. Its surround, and indeed all the other interior walls, had been slovenly painted black.

'Plenty of space,' Coates said. 'The outfit who were here were a slide-module company Pro-AV. I think they used in here as a combined boardroom and viewing theatre, I suppose you'd call it.'

'It's not the space. It's the light that's problematic,' Ethan said. 'Could I see it with the big door open?'

Coates blinked his eyes tightly shut but managed not to grimace.

'The big door isn't electric,' he said.

'But it does open ... '

'Of course. I don't know when it was last used, mind you.'

Coates moved to left and right of the door and withdrew

bolts. He caught hold of the rope dangling down from inside the top of the door and more in hope, it seemed, than confident expectation, pulled at it. Successfully. More easily than Ethan had imagined it would. The door glided inwards and upwards. Along with a welcome influx of fresh air, light flooded into the forward half of the big space eclipsing the thin, lacklustre illumination of the flossies.

'Excellent,' Ethan said. 'All the difference.'

'No problem,' Coates said, his relief evident.

'I think I'll probably take it,' Ethan said. 'Just let me sleep on it for twenty-four hours and do a few sums.'

'Of course.'

'I'll let you know one way or another tomorrow.'

'It's a snip at the price,' Ethan said, 'and it's literally within walking distance. It even comes with off-street parking. Mind you, taking it on will relegate my support of Charlton to the long range. I'll end up only going across for the crunch fixtures.'

'Not the first time Charlton have been relegated,' Ginny said.

'Careful!'

'There's always Queens Park Rangers.'

'Do you mind! Not worth the cost in shoe leather.'

'Well, anyway, if it gets you out of having to slog halfway across London every time you want to get serious with a brush, it's going to be cheap at half the price. Double the price. It'll add another two or three hours to your working day. Or sleeping nights.'

'Well that's sort of it, isn't it?'

'What is?'

'Working. I mean I'm not, am I? The money I got for "Box Hill" has gone and I ... well, I ought to be trying to lay the foundation for a grown-up professional career.'

'That's it. A solid base. You can't do that without a body of work to show.'

'Hawk about you mean. Look, there are gallery owners I know, contacts of a sort but – well, right now to get in round the corner we're looking at four hundred pounds.'

'Chicken feed.'

'Not to me. Not yet.'

'Ethan, what's mine is yours. You know that. If it makes you feel nobler about it all, let's say it's just a loan. When you hit it big – as you will – you'll pay me back. Right now it's just for start-up.'

'Well – '

'Shut up and come to bed.'

Thus had begun several days of shirt-sleeves-rolled-up activity. He had signed on the dotted line for Unit 17. He had sent Mrs Henderson a final cheque and sourcing a Renault Traffic from a Shepherd's Bush van rental outfit sweated out the outraging fortunes of the Old Kent Road's stop-go insults. It had taken him less time to stow his minimal personal items into the van than his easel, work-table, tools, books and assorted completed and unfinished paintings and sketches. When emptied and cleaned up his erstwhile tip of a makeshift studio looked smaller than when full. Standing in the doorway he took a last lingering look around the vacancy he had created. This was where, finding himself, he had acknowledged his vocation and, in sharpening his craft, perhaps found a deeper self-respect. But that was yesterday.

Move on now. He would leave the imminently defunct television behind.

The Old Kent Road again survived, he claimed possession of his new studio by unloading his humble cargo indiscriminately in its larger section, then, done and dusted in a working day, shot the van back to the rental centre. He was back in what he must now regard as his 'home' before Ginny had returned from work.

'Good day?' she asked when she came in.

'Mission accomplished,' he replied. 'I've even peeled some potatoes.'

As ever, work begat work. Ginny was right. He needed to extend his portfolio. While he was in these parts it would be folly bordering on insanity not to crack on with his proposed Picturesque series. Battersea Power Station was only a hop, skip, and a jump away.

By day, at first, he drew various sketches of the shamefully neglected ruin. He crossed over to the north bank of the Thames to view the site from across the water. He decided to cheat. In a manner entirely at one with traditions of the Picturesque school, he would bring the power station closer to the river and, eliminating all foreground, exploit the moonlight twice over by reflecting it on the surface of the water. Further, he would turn the power station on its axis, thus to reveal the magnificent chimneys almost in line astern, defiant and enduring in his painting as they had been historically, and seeming to say they had been built by a finer race of men than those who now ignored them. He was on this north bank, beginning seriously to manufacture his design, when his mobile rang.

'Hello?'

'Ethan? Alec Bradley.'

'Ah, hello, Alec.'

'I gather I've phoned you at work. Sorry if I'm interrupting.'

'You've done it now. What's up?'

'I've had DI Carter on the line.'

'Yes, yes. What's her problem?'

'Miss Watson seems to have gone walkabout.'

'Who?'

'Emily. Emily Watson. Secretary and whatever to the late lamented Rupert Penrith.'

'Oh, her. Yes. Not Penrith's "whatever" I'm pretty certain.'

'She's gone completely AWOL. Right off the map. In terms of the inquest that's a criminal offence technically.'

'Technically?'

'Assuming you turn up and don't do a runner yourself, her evidence is neither here nor there.'

'So not really a problem, then?'

'Not for the coroner. But maybe for DI Carter. To date her investigation still hasn't got five eighths of bugger all.'

'No?'

'There was no forced entry into Dorset Street that evening. Someone had to have let whoever it was in. It could have been Penrith himself, of course, or it could have been little Miss Watson.'

'They could just have walked in straight off the street through an open door.'

'Unlikely given the sort of place it was and at that time of evening, wouldn't you say?'

'Hmm ... Maybe.'

'Anyways, Carter would like to question said Emily again: ask her to confirm what time she left that Friday and so on. Who looked in that afternoon. Probably not so significant but you never know.'

'She can't just have vanished into thin air.'

'She's not been seen at her flat – Finsbury Park – for at least a week. Not visited her mum in Bristol – father's dead – nor her sister in Norwich. As I say, it's not the end of the world inquest-wise as long as you show up – '

'As I will.'

' – but, off the record, any idea where she might be would be gold dust for Carter.'

'Not a clue. Sorry, but I hardly knew her.'

'OK, not to worry. Just thought I'd ask the question. Doesn't look too good on Carter's CV you understand to let her go AWOL.'

'But it does look sinister.'

'Certainly. But never mind, eh? Sorry to have butted in on your working day.'

Click.

It never rains but it pours; wait half an hour at a stop for a bus to arrive and then three roll up nose to tail. So it is with inquests, Ethan Shaw discovered. On two successive days, the Post Office earning its dearly paid for corn by forwarding his correspondence on, he received essentially identical letters insisting on his presence at the respective inquests into the deaths of Messrs. Penrith and Marsh. The former to take place not in the Ealing Studios film set he had imagined it would be, but in a commandeered Court of Appeal within spitting distance – so convenient for the learned friends – of Harrod's back entrance. The latter inquest was held in Barnes in what, unfurnished, might have usually served as a territorial reserve army drill hall.

He duly turned up at both venues and twice briefly

corroborated the facts as stated by the policeman preceding him. On both occasions he was thanked by the coroners, one male one female, for his succinctness and both commiserated with him at his misfortune in having stumbled upon two such gristly happenings, one vertical, the other horizontal. This official sympathy was delivered in both cases in so routinely laconic a form of institutional wording, he would have preferred it to have been left unsaid. The respective verdicts were the foregone conclusions: suicide while the balance of mind was disturbed and, since DI Carter and her team had turned up diddley-squat ('several lines of investigation are being rigorously pursued'), murder by a person or persons unknown.

As he was crossing the vestibule or the Knightsbridge courthouse on his way out, he sensed someone at his shoulder. Without turning his head, before a word was spoken, he knew who it would be.

'No surprises there,' said DI Bradley.

Or here either, Ethan thought.

'Cul-de-sac case so far,' Bradley went on. 'Still the planting can go ahead now, anyway.'

'Or cremation.'

'No, he was a left-footer, remember. There'll be a service. Any thought of attending?'

'No. None at all.'

They had come down some steps on to the London pavement. Bradley had halted, abruptly obliging Ethan to turn inwards and face him. Head on one side, the worry lines on his forehead clear in the bright light, Bradley squinted upwards and sideways.

'Might be an idea if you did,' he said.

'I didn't really know him.'

'You were on his payroll when he went to meet his Maker.'

'Was despatched you mean.'

'Either way, it would be seemly.'

'Crocodile tears time. His people haven't the faintest idea who I am.'

'There's his partner. Walsh. You could contact him and ask for a ticket. They'll be going free, I imagine.'

'What's the point?'

'Your profession has given you sharp eyes. If you go, you might hear and notice something. Something we plods wouldn't hear or see.'

Bradley's tone was once again more urgent, more loaded, than that used by a man offering to buy a mate another pint. Ethan shrugged his exasperated and reluctant understanding.

'It doesn't end, does it?' he said.

'It never does,' Bradley agreed.

9

AS NO DOUBT DEMANDED BY ITS school charter the chapel at Ardleigh was exclusively dedicated to Catholics. Nevertheless, topography had contrived to make it something of a broad church. It flanked the entire northern side of the small, grassed quadrangle that was the centre of the classrooms, dormitories, school hall, library, gymnasium and so forth that made up the overall Ardleigh complex. When, having flourished his formal printed invitation at some sergeant-like porter figure at the western entry, Ethan entered the chapel, he discovered at once that the building was very nearly as wide as it was long. A shortish central nave extended directly before him towards the altar: but, presumably to accommodate the entire schoolboy population, the Victorian architect had made provision for two further sets of pews in what were in effect parallel, if shorter naves that ran to its left and right. All three naves had their own vaulted roof and were separated not only by aisles but by squat, somewhat ugly, weight-bearing pillars. The overall effect, Ethan almost immediately concluded, was one of hugger-mugger crowded disunity. Quickly he sat himself down in the back row of the furthest left set of pews. He was inside now, ticked off on the sergeant major's list. He could watch well enough from here.

Beyond three banks of execrably rendered stained glass windows aft of the altar at the eastern end, there wasn't much worth looking at. The chapel was going to be lamentably under-filled. The struggle of other mourners entering after him – middle-aged or elderly to a man and woman, slightly self-conscious in their unfamiliar mourning suits – was only going to fill the first four or five rows of the central pews. He didn't know any one of them from the utterly awful Adam in the far window. A scuffing of leather caught his ear and a flurry of movement the corner of his eye. He turned his head. Indifferent, it seemed, to the gap they were creating between themselves and everybody else, three men had settled down at the very rear of the central nave.

Now there was someone he could recognise. The central one of the three was Khalid Nahkla, race-horse owner and authenticated billionaire. As seen on TV. Also, not least, the sole authenticated person he had ever sold a painting to. A handsome man, to go by his profile – middle-aged, his short, conventionally parted hair was flecked with gravitas-conferring grey, his skull neatly rounded and in proportion to the broad shoulders. His complexion was what would be most interesting to paint. Nahkla's unbearded features almost glowed. The skin was the lightest tan – tan with a suggestion of gold.

The two men flanking him were white and European. Bulkier still, both dark-haired in a short-back-and-sides way, they had to be minders. Yes, clearly. Their body language showed them to be on the *qui vive* all the time. You could almost see the guns in their shoulder-holsters. Suddenly his interest quickened. It was the man nearest to him he would really like to paint. As this man's head moved to look at something, he had unwittingly demonstrated that he had the most amazing profile.

Essentially he had no nose. Seemed not to have one. Maybe he had once been a boxer and had had his original hooter smeared off his face. Where you'd expect a bridge, a protruberance, something convex, there seemed to be only a vacancy, negative space. Whatever was between the man's eyes was shallower than a politician's election pledge. Tricky things noses, their bones very close to the brain. Perhaps some surgeon had decided to sing a song of sixpence rather than re-set a dodgy nose bone. Careful. In its ceaseless monitoring of the chapel the man's curious head was beginning to turn his way. Ethan glanced down quickly at the order of service he still held.

An organ began to play stealthily, creepily. Almost at once it was half-drowned out by a cacophony of scraping, clanging and banging from the direction of what passed for the chapel's chancel. Lead by a priest who must have selected the most unassuming of his surplices from his wardrobe that morning, the coffin was being processed down one off-centre aisle by the undertakers' strong-arm men. Everybody was getting to their feet so, a trifle belatedly, Ethan did too. He was unable to prevent himself wondering whether the severed hand had been tucked into the coffin as an afterthought or would be along shortly in a little box of its own. Behind the coffin walked only a single person – a very tall heron-like figure. This surely had to be Leonard Walsh. If ever a man looked as his voice over the phone had suggested he might, this was he. At the end of the aisle Walsh side-stepped into the front pew, the priest said something, the bearers lowered the coffin on to some pre-positioned trestle. Completely disinterestedly they marched back up the chapel and out. Job done and dusted for the time being. Facing the thirty or so mourners the priest began to speak. Inaudibly.

From his position right at the rear of the chapel, Ethan could not make out if the priest were mumbling in English or Latin. When he had phoned to obtain an invitation to the ceremony, Walsh, in a voice high-pitched and querulous (and, indeed, thinking it over, heron-like) had first questioned him suspiciously as to his *bona fides* and then informed him that the service would be 'a requiem mass but not a full one'. He had no idea what that meant and the quite skimpy 'programme' of the order of service offered no clue. Anyway, there the priest was gesturing and, wham!, now his ears were being assailed by the tones of an invisible woman blasting at him from a hidden source.

This, the order of service told him, was Margaret Willoughby, Penrith's elder sister. As over-microphoned as the Monsignor was not, she must be speaking from some kind of lectern arrangement completely blocked from view by one or other of the ungainly columns. She, he could tell only too well, was speaking English.

During the following interminable ten minutes he learned about Penrith the things he had already learnt about the deceased at the only two funerals he had to date previously attended: Penrith had been possessed of a uniquely wonderful sense of humour; he had been the apple of his parents' eyes; in later years he had been the linchpin of the extended Penrith family, never missing a birthday in his despatch of greeting cards; he had adored Marmite; he was a grievous loss and, being sorely missed, would always be lovingly remembered.

Margaret Willoughby made no mention of her brother having been a somewhat craven-hearted swindler and, perhaps wisely, failed in conclusion to comment upon the manner in which he had been obliged to quit this world.

Still officiating without benefit of amplification the priest possibly made further remark of a complimentary and even sacred nature and then the people in the forward pews were getting to their feet *en masse*. Safety in numbers. Ethan stood up as well. The order of service seemed to indicate a hymn; words were printed. They were also English but he didn't recognise them in this combination. Nor, when the organ struck in, did he recognise the tune. He almost did, but the organ, insisting upon descanting twiddly little bits, was obliterating the top line. Better not to sing at all. He stood gold-fishing away while the organ left the ad hoc choir before the altar floundering in its wake. The organist found a possible final chord. It was sufficient to bring Leonard Walsh stalking forward to eclipse himself behind another intervening pillar.

This time there were items of mild interest. This memorial service was taking place at Ardleigh because here was where Rupert had spent his always cherished school days and where the two of them had met and grown to know each other. Rupert had been celebrated throughout the school for his infectious sense of humour.

He had, in early days, been a mainstay of the choir here in this very chapel and soloist of choice whenever a recital of any public nature was undertaken. Rupert had three times won the Hudson prize for an original painting and the designs he had executed for the sets and costumes of the Ardleigh production of *The Merchant of Venice* were remembered by some to this day. Leaving school, Rupert had eventually found a place at Bonhams; one of the coups he had pulled off there had been his ferreting out a small early Poussin from a shop more junk than antique in Brighton. It had been this discovery that had encouraged him to set up in business as a dealer in his own right and his underwriting any transaction was a guarantee of its probity. It was perhaps a pity that Rupert had not shown similar powers of discrimination in matters of horseflesh but all the same, if not financial gain, he had derived enormous pleasure from the sport of kings. It was in Life itself that he had occupied the Winners' Enclosure.

The heron stalked back to his seat. The rest would presumably be silent. The Monsignor was handling a chalice, his lips moving. Ethan worked out that Communion was about to be celebrated. This, for him at least, held novelty. The priest's lips continued to move. He was giving the impression of having a routine gossip with his deity as to the nature of the motley crew that had invaded their precincts this morning. Now, though, cup in hand, he was approaching the altar rail.

Most of the foreground group were again on their feet. A few visibly partook of the body and blood of Christ. Most, however, forearms crossed over their chests like a cricket umpire rescinding his original decision following television review, sought no more than, he hazily recalled, the lesser gift of a blessing. He himself, of course, could not aspire even to that. But – the last of them was sitting down again – he might hope for relief. Like himself, Nahkla and his minders had not moved a muscle.

Light and cold air flooded into the chapel. On some invisible cue the undertakers' men were marching back down the aisle like particularly well-drilled pickets. They had the coffin aloft. They were shouldering it. He remembered to stand as it drew level with his row. It had passed, was gone. The organ began to fugue away. Perhaps somewhere in all that the priest had managed to bless the deceased and commend his soul to its Maker. God would know.

While people shuffled towards and out through the main

entrance, Ethan stayed put where he sat. Nahkla and Co must have been among the first to leave. That pew was now empty. A wasted day. There had been nothing he had seen, heard or, certainly lip-read, that would be grist to DI Carter or Bradley's mill. His best bet now would be to find a decent pub.

He left the chapel last of all. Shifting nervously from foot to foot, some even on the quadrangle grass, people were standing about in knots of three or four. Now ... this was close to Reading ... what would be the local brewery in these here parts ... ?

'Mr Shaw!'

A crisp and very pukka voice had called out his name from behind his left shoulder. Turning, he saw Khalid Nahkla striding purposefully towards him along the gravelled border. A metre behind him strode his two minders walking side by side. But they had undergone a strange metamorphosis. Instead of the protection offered by two best of British rugby forwards, Nahkla was now in the care of two tall, thin attendants with skin as copper-gold in colour as his own. In advance, smiling easily, he proffered his right hand. Ethan clasped it – a firm, no-nonsense grip – on reflex.

'I knew it had to be you,' Nahkla was saying. 'Leonard told me you would be here today and no-one else is young enough – Khalid Nahkla,' he confirmed.

'How do you do? I did recognise you – from photographs. But I didn't want to intrude. I wasn't sure whether – '

'You didn't wish to seem pushy on a day like today. I quite understand. But you shouldn't have worried.'

'I'm really glad you broke the ice. You occupy a unique position in my life. You're the only person on the planet I've ever sold a painting to.'

'Not the last, I'm sure. Anyway, you're already ahead of Van Gogh.'

'Not in all respects.'

Nahkla smiled in a manner that could have been taken for spontaneous. His two lieutenants did not. Implausibly handsome, they stood a respectful two paces to the rear and might or might not have understood every word. Their lustrous, never blinking eyes could have been staring at nothing.

'At all events,' Nahkla said, 'as yet you have time on your side. Unlike poor Rupert. You're not going on to the interment? I am. I'll have to be off any moment once Leonard's sorted out the transport.'

'No, I won't be going. To be perfectly candid I nearly didn't come at all.'

'Oh?'

'It's been a sort of poor man's *noblesse oblige* my coming. I scarcely knew Mr Penrith at all. But technically I was on his payroll when he was killed. So – '

'Very commendable. It was a terrible shock, of course.'

'It certainly was.'

'For you in particular. You found him, I understand.'

'Yes.'

'That must have been ... well. It was a strange sort of shock for me too. It was very eerie hearing the news out in the Gulf. In the Kingdom. It was totally surreal. Like a mirage. I jumped straight into my plane and flew back thinking, "No, it hasn't happened and when I touch down I'll find he's still alive." Not, alas, the case.'

'Er ... '

'You seem taken aback.'

'I am, actually. Your plane?'

'I've got two planes. Lear Jets. One I keep here at Kidlington; the other in the States at Burbank. My greatest pleasure in life these days is piloting my way across the Western Hemisphere. Does that strike you as excessive?'

'Not if you can afford it. A touch risky, maybe.'

'Now, now. I spent two years at Cranwell after I left here. I have my licences. Fixed wing and helicopter. Yes, I was here too, you know. A few years behind Rupert. Here's where we first met. Then for years – nothing ... Then, quite by chance, we bumped into each other at Lingfield. Both wearing the old school tie, would you believe? I shall truly miss him. But at least he drew my attention to your watercolour.'

'Well – '

'I can't tell you what pleasure it's giving me. So quintessentially English. So green and pleasant. I'm going to ship it over to my home in Palm Springs, you know. I'll hang it there. Then, when the air-conditioning becomes intolerable I'll look at it and soothe my eyes and imagine myself drinking in great gulps of good old moist and grassy English air.'

'Khalid!' The high and querulous voice could also shout from afar.

'Ah, duty calls. Well – '

'Mr Nahkla. If, that is – '

'Yes, of course. Just plain "Mister".'

'Before you go, could you please explain your conjuring trick to me?'

'My conjuring trick?'

'Your associates. In the chapel you had Tweedledum and Tweedledee whereas here you have – '

'I have Ali and Abu – ' Khalid Nahkla laughed as if he might be amused.

'Yes.'

'Well, you see, Ali and Abu come of the true faith. A Catholic chapel is not, shall we say, quite their cup of tea. Sometimes if it is felt necessary to sheepdog me, certain parties interested in my wellbeing are obliged to make alternative arrangements.'

'Er ... '

'Khalid!'

'You'll miss the cortege.'

'They will wait for me. Let me first anticipate your question. I was a very early convert. When I was six I was sent to a school in Alexandria, Victoria College, modelled on English public school lines and run by Jesuits. Then in my early teens I came here. Forgive me, I should go now. This has been a pleasure. We'll talk again.'

He had turned away and gone. His two Arab minders, whatever their real names were, had followed at his heels like faithful pointers. Borzois, rather, Afghans. The contrast could not have been more marked. Where the pale, pasty-faced Tweedledum had had that alcove of a nose, Tweedle-Abu, or perhaps Ali, was possessor of a rampant scimitar that seemed exuberantly to challenge the world to take him on.

Everyone had marched off now. God – whichever God – he could murder a pint!

10

SO PENRITH AND MARSH WERE GONE; but for those left behind life went on. And so too, of necessity, did work. For Ethan Shaw, rising thirty, the daunting realisation that, for someone pursuing so nebulous a career as that of an artist, the boundary between self-employment and unemployment was non-existent when it came to income, bulked up more intimidatingly every fresh day he awoke. He wasn't in the Army now. He was out on his own and virtually a kept man.

He sought hard to create a career path. Fatiguingly he went the round of art-gallery shops and in two instances managed to lodge examples – both landscapes – of his better work in outlets in Notting Hill and Camden.

'What I've really got to do,' he said one evening when, weary, he had returned to Hammersmith, 'is fix in my mind which strings to my bow I should cut loose. I can't go on faffing about between portraits and landscapes. I need to focus on the one and specialise.'

'To put it at the lowest level,' Ginny said, 'portraiture has to be where the money is.'

'Probably.'

'And you've always said that portraits were what attracted you most. And you know you're good at them.'

'In the meantime I've discovered it wouldn't be a bad idea to have a business card.'

'Well you can do that yourself. Design one anyway.'

'I suppose.'

'A better idea might be to set up a website. You could do that yourself too. Just find some IT whizz-kid and get yourself a shop window.'

'First I need a fuller portfolio.'

'Well, how about a portrait of me? That won't cost you anything.'

'I've often thought about that but I'm so much into you, I'm not sure I could ever do you justice. Or myself.'

'Well, there's only one way to find out.'

'All right. I should have suggested it yonks ago. Just let me get my Battersea Power Station out of the way first.'

After two false starts in translating his sketchbook material onto a large canvas, he had at last found the manipulated angle of the building and its unauthentic juxtapositioning with the Thames he had been after. It was with this sleight of hand that he had most successfully christened the unit he'd taken over as his new studio. He had charcoaled home the broad lines of the painting to be on the new canvas he'd expensively acquired when it came on to rain and an incessant drizzle had ensued. Straightaway he had taken himself off to the unit and, opening the large up and over door, set up his easel just inside the wide threshold. He was perfectly dry there and the light could not have been better. He got on like a house on fire – so much so that he felt he must be making a fool of himself, must be overlooking something crucial. He backed off from the easel to take stock. No – this was what he had intended. It had been right to ignore the corny idea of invisibly igniting the power station's furnaces to allow clouds of smoke to billow from the chimneys. He might have achieved some interesting touches by highlighting the clouds with the moonlight but he was after something more austere than cheap melodrama. And that floating idea he'd had of painting the London Eye by night – that had to be a too theatrical no-go area also; he was not about to set himself up as a purveyor of High Street kitsch.

That evening, waiting well beyond sunset and knowing there would be a nearly full moon, he returned to the further side of the Thames across from Battersea to reconsider how he would handle the river. The conditions were perfect for his purpose, the sky without a cloud, the moonlight skating brilliantly on what might have been a river of mercury. Abruptly, his phone had bleeped and he had known it had to be Bradley.

'Hello?'

'Do I find myself talking to Mr Shaw?'

Not Bradley. A cultured BBC-ish voice that he simultaneously knew he recognised but there in the chill night wouldn't be able to identify.

'Er, yes ... '

'Khalid Nahkla speaking – '

'Ah yes! Of course! Ardleigh. Sorry, I didn't – '

'Am I disturbing you? Interrupting you?'

'No. No not at all. I'm just taking a walk, actually.'

'Yes. The weather's cleared up nicely has it not? When we parted company down at Ardleigh I said that I hoped our paths would cross again and in fact something cropped up that very day which makes our meeting particularly desirable. From your point of view perhaps professionally desirable.'

So. He had a profession after all, did he?

'Oh?'

'I wonder whether we might indeed meet? I know it's devilish short notice but I do find myself in London tomorrow morning and it would be ultra-convenient if you could drop in then. You and your sketchpad, I might say.'

'My sketchpad?'

'It's a bit too complicated for the phone. Better gone into face-to-face. I can promise it will be almost certainly worth your while.'

'It happens that I do have a free morning tomorrow.'

'Good. Shall I tell you where to find me?'

'Please.'

'I have a little *pied á terre* in the Waterside Tower immediately west of Battersea Park. Do you know it?'

Of all the gin joints! He could see it from where he was standing. They could almost be having the conversation without benefit of phone.

'I do know it,' he said. 'I've had no occasion to go there but I do know it. We're talking about the Thames' south bank, aren't we?'

'Indeed. Could you manage eleven o'clock?'

'That sounds very civilised. I can indeed.'

'Excellent. Parking's not a problem. But if anyone gives you trouble just mention my name.'

'Copy that. How did you get my number, by the way?'

'Oh – from Leonard Walsh.'

Had that been a slight hesitation or had he imagined it?'

'I rang the Dorset Street Gallery chasing after you and, by good fortune, Leonard picked up himself. He's selling on the lease, you know, and letting Sotheby's auction off what stock Rupert still had on his hands.'

Hand, actually.

'He gave me your number. Along with a few kind words.'

'Who's taking the premises over.'

'I don't know. Presumably not a tattooist, given the area.'

'Hardly. Quite likely another dealer.'

'A jeweller, perhaps. There's still quite a chunk of time outstanding on the lease ... '

'Well ... Tomorrow at eleven, then. The Waterside Tower?'

'Indeed. There's a concierge on 24-7 duty there. He'll let you know how to find me. I'll look forward to it.'

'As will I.'

'Don't forget your pad. Enjoy the rest of your walk.'

A patrician farewell, just a little less than condescending. I have the politeness to remember your small-talk. Or perhaps he was just well mannered.

The evening had been snapped in two. But it didn't matter. Looking at the river now, the moon ennobling it with that shimmer which he could incorporate into the foreground of his composition, he felt relaxed. A dark tug, towing two even darker barges in its wake, was taking advantage of the ebbing current to nose downstream and breaking the bright sheen upon the black water into interestingly patterned kaleidoscopic fragments. But the surface of his painted Thames would be intact and unruffled. This again would be an instance where less would be more. He should know, shouldn't he? He was a professional now.

The next morning Ethan drove south of the river over Battersea bridge and then turned left towards the park. Turning left again he zig-zagged his way back towards the river through a series of undistinguished and minor side streets and then – lo and behold – caught sight of a vacant kerbside parking space in the unmetred street. Seize the day! He slotted his Toyota home and rejoiced at having killed two birds with one stone. First, anxious, he had set out absurdly ahead of sensible time. Now he could sit quietly here a few minutes and time his arrival to the cool split-second. Second, he had lanced a mental boil that had been nagging him all morning. The Waterside Tower had regularly made the news in the past few years as the London residence of various flash Members of Parliament, louche entrepreneur wheeler-dealers and former pop stars now settling for long-in-the-tooth retirement on their ill-gotten gains. The parties held there still occasionally rioted over the top to attract snapping paparazzi to its forecourt. He'd had qualms about arriving in that same forecourt in his ancient pile of rust-bucket junk and parking it alongside the Porsches and Jaguars that were sure to be congregated all about. Even from the highest storeys his poor man's wheels would stand out like a tainted cell in a brain scan. But now, his car left here, he could approach this citadel of bling anonymously on foot.

As befitted a peasant calling in on a billion – rather than million – aire, he had dressed smart-casual: his best (since only) sports jacket and, to show he'd given his appearance no thought whatsoever, his best, immaculately laundered old jeans. He wore no tie but the crisp blue work-shirt of a labourer worthy of his hire. Whatever he wore, Nahkla would know him for a pauper at a glance.

Still, as he drew near the Tower he was glad he had made the effort to dress casually up. Approached on foot, the building ceased to be just another high-rise council flats, head offices, first timers' apartments – that you saw all the time out of the corner of your eye as you drove around London. Focused upon stand-alone fashion it began to take on individual personality – a personality whose keynote seemed one of weary, money-bags disdain.

For a start, its basic structure was not made up of pre-cast concrete slabbed into place but of standard sized bricks in a subdued but pleasant red-brown colour and able to eschew all recourse to cladding. The labour cost in manpower implicit in laying them one on top of the other must have been phenomenal but the quality of the brushed steel framing to the spread of picture windows seemed commensurate. From the second storey up to – he counted them – the fourteenth, graceful, generously proportioned balconies in the same steel indicated the division and number of apartments to each floor. Those on the further side must command views of the river.

He had done well to ditch his car. A private service road led down to a carparking area where heavy metal was indeed displayed in serious money profusion. A couple of Bentleys, even. But first, if you wanted access, a check-point Charlie had to be negotiated. As he walked towards it, it didn't appear to be manned, a top-of-the-range Lexus purred past towards the barrier and, untouched by human hand, probably activated electronically by some gismo pre-mounted in the vehicle, the barber shop pole duly rose in salute to let the fat cat through. A slow count of six and as quietly as proverbial paint drying it had lowered itself back to the horizontal.

Ethan sidled past the end of the high-tech barrier rather expecting sirens to signpost him as an interloper, but silence prevailed. Not smiling, although he could be sure he was on CCTV, he walked down a slightly inclined downward slope towards the Tower's entry doors. These were not massive but made entirely of glass and subtly tinted glass at that. As he neared them the one door slid easily behind the other and he was able to walk straight on into the vestibule without breaking his stride.

The vestibule was not vast but, broader than deep, rectangular. In the centre of its tiled floor was a mosaic which in mid-blue outlined the London course of the Thames and so inevitably put him in mind of *Eastenders*. Perhaps the purpose was to remind the denizens of this monument to Mammon how the other half lived and that they should count the blessings of their West End lifestyle. To the right of the vestibule as he entered was an extensive low-slung counter-desk. Behind it sat a man whose aura of hostile deference made the legend CONCIERGE on the baton on the desktop immediately in front of him thoroughly redundant.

'May I help you, sir?' the man immediately intoned.

Ethan looked at him. He was wearing no uniform but an expensive-looking brass-buttoned blazer and a tie that was either club or regimental. He was probably in his mid-fifties. He had a pinkish complexion with a sprinkling of drinkers' veins about his sharp cheek bones, a tight mouth, tighter eyes and short silver hair parted and brushed in no-nonsense 1940ish style. He reminded Ethan of a Sergeant-Major he had endured in Belfast.

'Ethan Shaw to see Khalid Nahkla,' Ethan said. 'I have an eleven o'clock appointment.'

The concierge nodded in a manner somehow reluctant and glanced down at the list on the sheet of paper right in front of him. He had a bank of six small television monitors to his left-hand side. One showed the checkpoint barber's pole and explained much. The concierge, meanwhile, had been making an ostentatious mark on his list.

'If you'd be good enough to go to the lifts in the far corner, sir,' he said, 'and take the one on the left, the small one, I'll let them know you're on your way up.'

'Thank you,' Ethan said as neutrally as he could manage and turned away in the indicated direction.

There was an illuminated button at the side of the narrow lift but before he had reached forward, the lift door slid open of itself. Force perforce he found himself entering a compartment that was indeed relatively small. Perhaps six adults standing upright and holding their breaths could have been accommodated for a short sardine tin ascent. Before he had definitively decided if this were so, the door, again unbidden, had closed behind him. The floor beneath his feet quivered for an instant and then as he clocked that the instrument panel contained not a bank of numbered buttons but merely two, a red and a green, he could not quite be certain that the lift was in motion. Apparently it had been because the floor had shimmied again. Surprising him, a door at the opposite end by which he had entered the compartment now opened behind him and, turning around, he stepped out to be confronted by still two more surprises.

The first was the general one that the lift had delivered him not to some kind of an external lobby area but into what was clearly the interior of someone's abode. So it must be with penthouse privileges. The particular surprise was that scrutinising him intently as the lift door closed automatically behind his back, was none other than Tweedle-Ali, or as it might be, Abu.

'Mr Shaw.' It was a statement rather than a question and proof already that Ali -Abu did not only understand English but spoke the language with a cut-glass accent.

'Indeed,' Ethan replied in his best up-market Received.

Ali-Abu coughed. He was staring fixedly at the large bag which, as was his custom and, indeed, as per his instructions, Ethan was carrying slung from his shoulder. He got the message immediately and without further words handed the satchel over.

'Tools of the trade,' he said. 'Sketching materials.'

Ali-Abu nodded. Swiftly and deftly but not casually he sifted the bag's contents. He was wearing a to-die-for linen suit, a carefully selected tan shade two tones darker than his own skin. A cocoa-brown silk tie drove home what a dandy its wearer was at heart. He didn't look the least bit like Lewis Carroll but, the bravura thrust of the beaked nose apart, a refined modification of the Valentino template. He was now confronting Ethan with raised eye-brows as he held aloft a paint bespattered Stanley Knife.

'For sharpening things – charcoal sticks, pencils,' Ethan said. 'Cutting things too. Paper, canvas. Not throats or windpipes.'

Without comment or reaction but with elegant economy Ali-Abu slid the knife into his jacket pocket.

'On the way out,' he said.

'Keep it,' Ethan tried with. 'I've got umpteen more back home.'

Ali-Abu's eyebrows rose higher.

'Such largesse,' he said. 'If you'd be so good as to follow me.'

He led the way down a corridor just long enough to contain a pair of doors to the left and the right and into a very large space which was flooded with a light that dazzled and bemused. It was like this Ethan realised, his eyes adjusting, because the side walls to the place, north and south, were continuous runs of glass. Further, none of the furniture in the penthouse lounge was taller than waist high. Nothing impeded the light.

Removing sunglasses, a figure was in motion at the far end of the space. Khalid Nahkla rising from a Charles Eames chair seemed to epitomise his surroundings. Like a champion tennis player advancing to the net to shake hands after yet another straight sets victory, he was trekking forward with his hand extended.

'Ethan,' he said, 'how nice. You found us then.'

'It does rather stand out,' Ethan said as they shook hands. How are you?'

Nahkla was smiling.

'So it does,' he said. 'Hard to miss. Come outside at once and get your bearings.'

He led the way across what seemed a leathered parquet floor to where, almost imperceptible to a first glance, a door was set into the glass of the north-facing window. He opened it and stepped forth on to an unfeasibly large balcony.

Ethan's ears did not quite pop but the sudden access of noise into the room along with the inward gust of breezy fresh air instantly told him how quiet, how noiseless the long room had been. Nahkla was gesturing his hand boyhood-of-Raleigh fashion in the direction of the north-west where, beyond the Thames right at their feet, it seemed, the sprawl of London stretched its way towards the Wembley Stadium arc.

'The Great Wen,' Nahkla quoted, and having somehow known in advance that this is what he would say, Ethan felt strangely comforted. The man was human, fallible, even commonplace.

'A surprising amount of greenery,' he said.

'Yes, isn't there? You don't notice it when you're down there part of it.'

Gingerly, Ethan edged forward to the balcony's outer edge. At once he felt uncomfortable. A slalom of vertigo had slithered through his brain. This height was terrifying. Still too connected to the ground below to make the downwards drop impersonal or insignificant. For an instant he felt the soles of his feet melting as he flirted mentally with the idea of flinging himself over the rail and into space. Just to see what it felt like. Would you be obliviously insane before you hurtled into the asphalt below? Would you pass out? Would the whole of your past life fast forward across your inner vision? Ugh! His stomach was roiling. He forced himself to concentrate on the bridges, Vauxhall, Battersea, now a shelf for mobile Dinky toys, Albert, of course, the one you always forgot ...

'We're just too far downstream to get the boat race,' Nahkla now said. 'But I can live with that. Horses apart, I've never been much into professional sport.'

Ethan nodded his agreement. The breeze blew strongly up here, probably always did. It was strikingly fume-free in its freshness.

'Oh, I say!' Nahkla said abruptly. 'I haven't offered you any refreshment. Coffee, perhaps?'

'Coffee would be just wonderful. The breeze up here makes you very aware of your senses, doesn't it?'

'Puts a real edge on your appetite, yes. After you.'

They went back inside. As Nahkla closed the door silence descended like an act of grace. Nahkla himself broke it.

'Ali!' he called out. That was that settled, then. And what décor! Now that his eyes had acclimatised, Ethan could discern that the sofas, low tables, sideboards and armchairs were not only deployed carefully to divide the space into various discrete areas but in a way that together with their inherent quality contrived to knock a Tottenham Court Road furniture display into a cocked hat. Not an ashtray misplaced, no two adjacent colours clashing, this effortless luxury managed to feel comfortably lived in and not excessive.

Ali had appeared from behind what Ethan now appreciated was a discontinuous false wall at the long room's western end. There must be other rooms back there, a kitchen, bedrooms, an office-study.

'Ali,' Nahkla said, 'coffee, if you'd be so kind.'

'There's some brewing, sir,' Ali answered nodding. 'How do you take yours, Mr Shaw?'

'Just black, no milk or sugar, please.'

Ali nodded again and was no longer there.

'Well, to business,' Nahkla said. 'Please have a seat.'

He had indicated an armchair tight against a light-wood side-table. An identical chair was set at a right-angle to the first. The two men sat as one.

'It's pleasant to be meeting in rather more amiable circumstances than those of our first encounter,' Nahkla said.

'I was rather underwhelmed by the morning, I must admit.'

Nahkla pulled a sour face and nodded.

'I have attended better laying-to-rests,' he said shortly. 'Things didn't improve at the actual interment. But afterwards, over the South African sherry and so forth, there was finally a positive side to the day.'

'Yes?'

'I got talking to the Chairman of the Ardleigh trustees and, well, to cut a long story sideways, I ended by agreeing to fund a much needed extension to the Ardleigh school library.'

'So how – '

'The almost ridiculous post-script to that is that, hugely grateful, of course, somewhat embarrassed, no doubt, the trustees have expressed their wish to have my portrait hung somewhere in the library entrance.'

'Ah – '

'The absurd illogic of their proposal – I've made enquiries – is that if they were to commission something from the current crop of, well, society painters, the fee they would have to stump up would come close to cancelling out the contribution I've undertaken to make.'

'Surely not. I can't tell – '

'So I thought of you. Poor Rupert did show me your rather good portrait of that very flakey MP who came to a sticky end not so very long ago and – '

'Yes. I completed that just days before he was killed.'

'Well. I liked it. I only saw it on a smart phone, of course, but I thought it caught something of the man's ambiguity.'

'Thank you. I worked hard to capture that. Mutton dressed up as lamb.'

'Exactly. How much will you ask for painting me?'

'You're not superstitious?'

'How do – Oh, I see. No. Lightning doesn't strike twice. How much to do me?'

'Er, one thousand pounds,' Ethan said and even as the syllables were passing his lips felt that the sum was absurdly too slight and simultaneously too ridiculously demanding.

'How does two thousand pounds sound?'

'Twice as good.'

'Then two thousand it will be then. It is understood the choice of artist rests with me. I'll write you a cheque today for five hundred to prime the pump and establish a contractual bond.'

Ali returned. On a no-nonsense wooden tray that might well have come from Ikea, he carried two white beakers, a white jug, and a Perspex one, filled to the brim with coffee.

He placed the tray down on the low table and, immediately filling the one beaker, handed it carefully across to Ethan along with a coaster and a linen napkin.

'Black, no sugar,' he tonelessly confirmed.

'Thank you.' Ethan replied in kind. The beaker, naturally, was porcelain, the aroma irresistible.

Ali was already attending to the second beaker. This time he only poured to halfway. Setting the Perspex jug back on the tray, he proceeded to top up the difference with stiff white cream from the milk jug which he dispensed via the back of a silver spoon. Probably the one that Nahkla had been born with, Ethan had time to reflect.

He'd let enough time elapse to demonstrate that he had been well brought up. He sipped his coffee. It was probably as good a cup as he could remember ever having tasted. French or Italian. He drank more vigorously and felt it sliding home. Ah ...

'Thank you, Ali,' Nahkla said.

Ali made himself scarce again. Miraculously, Nahkla had no trace of cream about his mouth. Time now to get back to business. *Alors ...*

Flushed through with euphoria at the prospect of re-employment, Ethan hated to be saying what he now heard himself saying.

'I'd be hugely keen to deliver a portrait study that pleases the trustees and does you justice,' he said. 'But there might be procedural problems. When am I going to get you to sit for me?'

'Yes. That could be tricky. I don't tend to stay in the UK for any great length of time these days. But that's a difficulty any artist taking me on would be faced with, obviously. How many sittings would you anticipate?'

'Not that many, actually. I could do some charcoal sketches now if you've got the time and – '

'Yes. Certainly.'

'And I'll take some photographs too – not to copy but for reference – and on the strength of that I can paint a pretty tight range-finding first stab.'

'Sounds good.'

'After that ... some weeks after, I'd need to grab you for a longish session. Three hours plus, I'd say.'

'That doesn't sound too dauntingly impossible.'

'Maybe then another long session. If I'm still struggling after that, well, it's probably abort time. A full refund if that occurs. All you'll have lost will be your time.'

'I've every confidence that won't come to pass.'

'Of course the big question is: how do you see yourself being done. Sitting? Full length and standing?'

'Oh, head and shoulders, I should think. Sitting I should imagine but not in the portrait. I've eaten too many indifferent meals in academic halls watched from the walls by anonymous old codgers stuffed into their Victorian chairs.'

'Well that's certainly good to hear. What about clothes?'

'How do you mean?'

'Academic gown? Lounge suit? Something Kuwaiti?'

'Good God, no! You're not dolling me up in Bedouin robes and putting a falcon on my wrist because I'm not a Bedouin and I'm not going to parade past future generations of Ardleighians as a cut-price Omar Sharif.'

'Sorry. I merely – '

'A suit should be just the ticket. Fairly informal. Something such as Ali is wearing today. Collar and tie, certainly. An Old Ardleighian tie, I suppose. That's a dark blue ground and a diagonal silver stripe.'

'Maybe make the suit grey-blue then.'

'Yes. That would do nicely. I've got several in that spectrum. Write me out your address and I'll arrange that a tie is sent along to you.'

'Fine.'

Ethan took his photos and then for the next three-quarters of an hour sketched full-faced and profile studies of his subject. It was not going to be the easiest of portraits to achieve, he realised. Ali with his so distinctive nose would have been easier. Khalid Nahkla with his very symmetrical, rather unexceptional, features would require the subtlest of handling. The trick would be to catch the forceful strength of purpose that lay just under the deceptively placid exterior. He should probably paint him smiling. The man had magnificent teeth.

'What about the background?' he asked.

'Well you decide. The library at Ardleigh has all the charisma of a third-rate Victorian town hall and the extension – I've chatted to the architect – is not going to be other than a four-square, brick-built pair of wings intended simply to supply utilitarian room for shelving and desks. There is talk of hanging the new portrait behind the central desk at the library's entrance.'

'Well then. Bog-standard though it is, perhaps I could paint you loud and clear, head and shoulders in the foreground, so to speak, of the composition and then indicate booklined shelves at some distance in the background. I'll paint them fuzzily like you get with out of focus photographs so, as well as gently echoing the actual library shelves, they will throw your own portrait into bolder, nearly three-dimensional relief.'

'Sounds good,' Nahkla said again. 'I'll leave it with you to try on for size and we can make a final decision later.'

'Yes, that will make sense.'

'You haven't given me your address yet.'

As he reached for a spare sheet of paper, Ethan tried not to hesitate and not let any concern show on his face. But he was concerned. All through the morning Ginny's interpretation of the shocking business of the severed hand had hovered on the edge of his consciousness. If she were right – it seemed so very plausible – Nahkla was the last person you would want saying to you: 'I know where you live.' But he wanted the commission and so had to have the tie. As he put pen to paper, inspiration guided his hand. The Post Office's forwarding service had not let him down yet and was set to run for three months. Well, then. Smoothly and naturally he wrote down his obsolescent Charlton address.

'My,' Nahkla said, 'You have come a distance.'

'It's not too bad once the rush-hour has died down.'

Abruptly and decisively Nahkla shot his cuffs and pointedly consulted his outrageously slim gold watch.

'Have all you need?' he asked as he rose to his feet.

'Yes. To be going on with. I think we're done for today,' Ethan found himself obliged to counter with. He too had stood.

The pair began to walk the long stretch back to the room's eastern end.

'One last thing before you go – I'd like to have your opinion on something,' Nahkla said. He had moved ahead to the clean-cut contemporary desk set at right angles to the picture windows which Ethan had entirely failed to notice on first entering, and was drawing open its single shallow drawer so as to take something out. A cardboard cylinder. He was removing a cap and teasing forth a roll of white paper. A scroll of some kind. As he began to unroll this, the light from the southern window was bright upon the right side of Nahkla's face. It emphasised the grey strands in his drawn tight hair and seemed to bring out the military commander in him. He was now laying some tissue paper aside and unscrolling paper more substantial. He flattened and spread this across the desk top and, seemingly as they just came to hand, weighted its corners down with an assortment of objects – a paper weight, an ink bottle, a magnifying glass, a slim polished grey and white stone.

'What's your opinion of this?' he asked.

It was a drawing, a sketch presented so that it was the right way round for his guest's point of view. When he was within five paces of the desk Ethan knew in general terms exactly what it was he was being asked to examine – a charcoal sketch of a racehorse, his jockey up, standing in profile with a groom or whomever at his head, long stirrups, onlookers behind the groom.

'Well,' Ethan began, 'obviously influenced by Stubbs. Might be a quick sketch of one of his paintings – early on, you know, he did several "pinup" sort of studies of celebrated horses for their proud owners. I don't know them well enough to say which one that might be. Of course I might be putting the cart before the racehorse; just possibly this might be a sketch Stubbs threw off in trying to decide upon a composition.'

'Do you think it might be?'

'Possibly ... '

Ethan bent forward and inserting his finger beneath a bare section of the paper rubbed it against his thumb.

'The paper's old,' he said. 'But you have to consider that the pose, the composition couldn't have been more than all in a day's work for Stubbs. A horse in profile – he would have had that locked home in his head the moment he laid eyes on the beast. Before even ... Perhaps he was trying the spectators on for size. The groom or trainer, perhaps, that woman, the crouching little boy ... They don't really work, do they? They clutter the composition up and unbalance it. If this is a preliminary sketch, I shouldn't think any of them survived into the final painting.'

'You don't think it's authentic, then?'

'I'm not really the person to ask. But if you were to hold a loaded gun to my head, I think I would have to say "No". Stubbs was trained as an anatomist. His drawings therefore are very precise ... tight ... Diagramaticalish. This. OK, it might have been thrown off in the heat of the moment, but I still think it's too loose. The wrong handwriting, if you see what I mean. If I'm remembering correctly Stubbs' line would have been more ... well, anatomical. And you see that bold, curved line outlining the horse's hind quarters?'

'Yes.'

'See how it's got a shadow?'

'Ah ... yes.'

'I think that's a misfire. The line peters out, zig-zags askew. It doesn't matter much in a quick sketch and the artist has smudged it into that shadow but I don't think Stubbs would have done it in the first place.'

It was true but hearing himself put it into so many words, Ethan hated himself for exploiting that moment when Kenneth Marsh must have realised his time at drawing board and easel was up.

'So you're saying it's not an authentic Stubbs? A forgery, in fact.'

'Push coming to shove, I would say "Yes". Someone might say it's the real thing – an idea Stubbs tried on for size but rejected, probably on account of the cluttered area, but you could counter-argue that is exactly what a cunning forger would be trying to make you think. But you need to ask an expert.'

'I already have. You're right.'

'Ah.'

'The paper is old. But not old enough. It's Victorian. Stubbs died in 1806.'

'I wonder when this one dates from, then?'

'Who can guess? Could you have come up with it?'

'No way. Not good enough a draftsman. Given a lot of midnight oil and rehearsals I might have managed something in the Degas manner. But even then not enough to fool an expert ... Is this yours now?'

'Unfortunately, yes.'

'How did you come by it?

'A friend drew my attention to it. He knew I was interested in racing.'

'Well ... it's a curio. Not altogether uninteresting.'

'Just not that real thing. I'd much rather have a full-colour blow-up of my Yellow Aster going first past the post at Epsom.'

'Well, the camera doesn't lie.'

'Whoever else does. As you said, I think we're done here, aren't we?'

Not so much a 'goodbye' as the field marshal dismissing a junior officer.

11

'GAINFUL EMPLOYMENT,' VIRGINIA SAID. 'WHAT A difference! Henceforth, if you want to you can clean your brushes in champagne.'

The skin-deep diversion of television banished to a black-screened never-never land, she and Ethan were cuddled together on the long grey sofa in the softly greyed living room. It should have been restful and tranquil to be chilling out there but Ethan could not help feeling that there was more to life than that.

'It's almost too good to be true,' he said.

'Why?'

'Well, why me? All that poppycock about the school trustees not being able to stump up for a top name artist. Money's absolutely no problem for Nahkla. He could have lobbed them another ten or fifteen grand as easily as coughing and let them commission a Timmerman or Belcito. That sort of petty cash is what he finds down the back of his sofa every weekend.'

'Don't you want to do it, then?'

'Of course I want to do it. He'll be a very interesting subject both as a general type and as an individual personality. What's more, I can do a good job on him. If I can match my portrait of your late lamented brother-in-law, I can see to it his isn't merely one more indistinguishable addition to that long line of fuddy-duddy commemorations of long forgotten big-wigs. With the wind in my favour, I can do better than that. Now, I know that. But he doesn't. Oh, he's muttered about seeing my work on a smart phone but that's nothing. He's got no earthly – '

Cutting him off in mid-worry the land line had rung.

'It's late but that will be Bradley getting back,' he said and picked up.

'Hello?'

'Ethan? Sorry to be calling this late but the day's been a right bugger.'

'Not to worry. Mine's been quite interesting.'

'Yeah? Look – I'm in a car parked up just round the corner from you. Any chance you can brief me eye-ball to eye-ball? I've got something pretty heavy for you. Maybe best not on the blower.'

'Why?'

'Well, you never know.'

'Really? All right, then. No problem.'

'Good. See you in a minute. I'll be arriving mob-handed, by the way. I've got some colleagues with me.'

'Ah ... '

'Be there in a jiffy.'

Click.

'Did you get that?' Ethan asked of Ginny. 'It was Bradley. He's favouring us with his presence. And with a posse.'

'Well now. How does he know which house to come to? I hope they don't think they're getting hot and cold running coffee.'

A jiffy turned out to be a rather extended and strained five minutes. It kept seeming as if the front door bell would sound but it didn't. Then, startlingly, it did. Ginny went to answer it and, left alone, Ethan heard a babble of overlapping voices in the hall that might have belonged to party-going guests. The living room door opened and, as he rose to his feet, Ginny entered leading a file of three others.

Alec Bradley was hard on Ginny's heels and behind him Jean Stafford. As they fanned out into the room, Ethan saw a second woman whom for a long split-second he failed to recognise. Then he did – DI Carter, who had questioned him at length in Dorset Street.

Ginny had gone over to the armchair at the back of the room.

'You three sit there,' she said, 'and you can pretend to be the three wise monkeys.'

'Would that were so,' Bradley said. The last to do so, he sat on the sofa between his two female colleagues.

'This meeting is quite irregular,' he said. 'It isn't happening.'

'Understood – I think,' Ethan said.

'Show me yours first,' Bradley said.

Sitting in the remaining armchair and as succinctly as he could, Ethan recounted his penthouse morning at Waterside Tower, dwelling in particular on the Stubbs forgery that Nahkla had asked him to examine. The three coppers listened to him without interrupting or exchanging glances. When he was finished, Bradley blew out his breath.

'Very interesting,' he said. 'And, I would think, circumstantially conclusive. Yes?'

He had addressed this short question to his left and right. Two short, sharp, decisive nods agreed with him.

'All right,' he went on. 'Our turn now. Gorgeous Gus is

no longer with us. He was found dead last night. Murdered.'

'Who?'

'That gorgeous Gus. Lord Blesdale. He was found in the woods at the far end of his little fourteen-acre back garden. He was lying on his back. Someone had very neatly placed his head on his chest. It was staring curiously at his feet.'

'God Almighty!' Ginny exclaimed.

'We're inclined to ascribe it to a human agency,' DI Carter said.

Stunned, Ethan sat lost for words. His blood seemed literally to be running cold and pooling in his stomach. He had not known Blesdale personally – merely glimpsed him in passing – but only as a very minor media personality. That public image had not been savoury. But all the same ... beheaded. Ginny was getting to her feet.

'I think I'll make some coffee,' she said. 'Black everyone?'

Everybody nodded.

'That would seem appropriate,' Bradley said as Ginny went out to the kitchen. 'What do you make of it all, Ethan?'

'You're the law in triplicate. Why ask me?'

'Because you're the artist.'

'Right ... Well, as you said just now – conclusive. I think it all hangs on that forged sketch Nahkla showed me. When Kenneth Marsh hung himself I told you that he'd told me that he knocked off one last Sexton that he reckoned wouldn't pass muster and that he'd told Penrith not to try anything on with it. But Penrith, I also reckon, was greedy and, as we know, needy. He went ahead regardless and tried palming the false Stubbs off on Nahkla on the strength of its subject matter – a racehorse. He thought Nahkla would indulge his passion and letting his heart rule his head, not have the nous to check on the sketch. He didn't really know his mark very well, did he? Nahkla did check – British Museum or wherever. The feedback was that Penrith had tried to stiff him. Big mistake.'

'A mistake in general,' Bradley said nodding, 'and a particular mistake to screw an acquaintanceship going back years. The two went all the way back to Ardleigh.'

'And Blesdale was there too,' DI Carter said suddenly.

'God knows what went on in the dorms after lights out. Nahkla was Penrith's junior,' Bradley said. 'Possibly fagged for him. And or Blesdale. A lot of vendetta material stored up there to fester through the decades, I shouldn't wonder.'

'Nahkla would have been lucky to get through the place without being called "wog" ten times a week,' Carter said with sudden savage bitterness.

'I think, Ethan,' Bradley said, 'Kenneth Marsh did himself a favour contriving his own exit. If he'd hung around – sorry – there would have been two hands in the pot.'

'Would they have known he was the artist?'

'Don't forget Penrith was worked over before his heart gave out. He'd have talked. Penrith was the sort who'd have fingered his own parents if it would get him a place on the Orphans' Outing. Carry on.'

'Well, Nahkla sussed he'd been bilked: proved it was so. He took his revenge out not only on Penrith but on the second man, I'm guessing, who had been an accomplice in the fraud – Blesdale. Marsh told me how it worked. You come up with a forgery and then, no matter how perfect its execution, you have to manufacture a provenance for it. Penrith would rope in some down-on-his-uppers, shady grandee – Blesdale is the type par excellence – and get him to swear blind the fake had been mouldering away in the family attic for generations. Who's going to doubt the word of a peer of the realm?'

'Any one with a couple of brain cells between their ears,' Carter spat out.

Ginny returned to the room carrying a tray laden with mugs and a coffee pot in a way that reminded Ethan of his morning. There hadn't been, mark you, a trace of blood or the slightest dishevelment on Ali's to-kill-for linen two-piece.

'I brought milk anyway,' Ginny was saying. She began to pour and serve. As she did, Ethan took the opportunity to scrutinise DI Carter more closely. He could forgive himself for almost forgetting her. Sitting opposite her on the tube he could easily have taken her for a mid-level professional – a chief librarian, perhaps, a pharmacist, an assistant head mistress. She was short and slight in build, her black hair straight and parted like a man's but reaching down over her ears down to the nape of her neck. This and her sharp, beaky face gave her the look of a back-garden bird. But perhaps sounded a warning note too. If she were questioning you on remand and you took her as a librarian, you would be making a very serious error of judgment.

'One severed hand, one severed head,' DI Carter now said, her speech when you thought about it sub-Lancastrianly sharp and matching her looks. 'It seem the two punishments are matching the same crime.'

'I was thinking about that in the kitchen,' Ginny said. 'I mean, I think I can claim credit for first suggesting cutting off a right hand was a Middle Eastern custom. Well, let's not forget that it seems the original idea was to maim Penrith – brand him, if you like – not kill him. It would have been a mark of contempt. For all the airs and graces he awarded himself Penrith was really a common little thief, as common as muck. His mutilation was designed to proclaim him as such to those with eyes to see for all the years he might live on.'

'So – Blesdale?' Jean Stafford asked.

'Ah,' Ginny went on, 'Blesdale you can agree, I think, played the lesser role in the Stubbs scam. And that would be true. And Blesdale, Gorgeous Gus, much as he would argue otherwise, was no gentleman. He was far too vainglorious, too anti-social, too much a Bullingdon thug to qualify as a gent. But what he was was a toff. The silver spoon never left his mouth. Anyone he came across he treated like dirt. But Nahkla is a toff too. I don't know about his pedigree but his money alone in this day and age gives him toff status too. Although, that said, if he and Blesdale ever knocked into each other in the royal enclosure at Ascot, I reckon Blesdale would privately have considered his lingering dollops of War of the Roses blood would have given him precedence over Nahkla and his tradesman's billions.'

'So what are you saying?' Bradley asked.

'Well, if we assume – as surely we have to – that Nahkla ... er ... engineered Gorgeous Gus's death, it was a case of toff versus toff. In a way Nahkla was paying Blesdale a tribute and treating him as an equal. He should die a nobleman's death. In another way he was putting the boot in: a man who breaks the gentleman's code should get it in the neck.'

'Ouch!' Jean Stafford said.

'Well personally, I buy that,' Bradley said. 'But it all remains hypothetical, doesn't it? We don't have an iota of hard evidence against Nahkla – not if he burns the Marsh fake. Marsh is dead, Penrith's dead, Blesdale is dead. The only witness that we could provide the prosecution with is Ethan here and it would be his word, however coherent, against a man able to afford the best defence team world-wide that money can buy. We've got nothing from Dorset Street, have we Rebecca?'

'Not a single, solitary thing,' DI Carter concisely put it. 'Five eights of bugger-all. And so far as I can make out long range from Leamington, there isn't the sniff of a lead in the Blesdale case either. They're not even sure where exactly he got the chop. In which case, there's something else.'

She looked sideways along the sofa at her two police colleagues.

'I haven't come out with this yet,' she said, 'but I might as well do it now. I can always deny it later. This morning the Chief Super called in and told me to close down the Penrith case.'

'What?!' Jean positively shouted.

'Yes really.'

'But there's been no time at all!'

'Don't I know it. But he told me right now we are overwhelmed with unsolved crimes and under-manning – which is true. And that being so we should fast-track the Dorset Street incident into cold-case status. He said cut our losses. Minimum family requiring closure, he said, no missing millions. So bin it. But I got that feeling we've all run into when it comes to top brass. The distinct impression there was something else he wasn't letting on about: a sense there was pressure downwards on him from higher up still.'

'That just isn't on,' Bradley snarled. 'Why do we bother? What's the point? You say he's come on like that before?'

'Yes.'

'When?'

'About eighteen months ago, we had a man shot dead on our patch. Body in an alley. Very neat job, back of the neck. Very professional. First indications were that it was Secret Service. Ours. We plain plods were told "don't go there; let it lie." So – What do you reckon?'

'As things now stand we couldn't charge Nahkla if he had form from here to Mecca,' Bradley said. 'So, justice apart, what's the difference?

'The difference might be,' Ginny burst out, 'that whether directly or indirectly, he's almost certainly the murderer whose portrait Ethan has contracted to paint.'

Bradley looked at Ethan.

'You can duck out of that, can't you?' he said.

'Who says I want to?' Ethan answered. He was conscious now that four pairs of eyes were trained on him.

'Not everyone gets the chance to paint a 22-carat genuine murderer,' he said. 'He's a fabulous subject and I know I can do a good job. He hasn't murdered me so far.'

'If it's true that trying to save his own skin Penrith let every cat out of the bag,' Ginny said, not without desperation, 'it's likely Nahkla knows you were pencilled in to take over from Marsh. Knows that you knew him.'

'I think that's pretty unlikely,' Ethan said. 'I'm certain when he showed me that dodgy Stubbs sketch, Nahkla was putting me to the test. He couldn't have known Marsh had put me wise on that one. In any case I told him it was a wrong 'un. I think that impressed him.'

Still the eight eyes stared at him.

'OK.' Bradley said. 'Nahkla may be an off-limits cul-de-sac to us mere plods but, all the same, if you're going to paint him you'll want to watch your back.'

'No way!' Ethan exclaimed. 'If I'm going to paint his portrait, I shall want to be looking at his front.'

12

OVER THE NEXT FOUR WEEKS ETHAN worked steadily, if intermittently, at his portrait of Nahkla. He did this exclusively at his new makeshift studio, which, he now found, suited his purpose very well. He came to enjoy and look forward to the very short walk from the house in Hammersmith to the industrial units site. In the ten minutes or so it took him he could sense himself narrowing his thoughts to concentrate on the painting. The dedicated studio put an edge on his mind and on his hands. When, finishing a session, he pulled down the main door and locked up, he could switch off. For a few hours overnight, his handiwork was out of sight and out of mind. He was not tempted to fiddle with it and spoil what was basically sound with after-thoughts.

He had chosen to paint Nahkla head on, giving the viewer an eye-line slightly lower, as it seemed, than that of the fractionally larger than life subject. Framed tightly, head and shoulders, Nahkla was to stare back intently at his viewer and seem, as in Ethan's experience he so often was, to be on the point of interrupting his interlocutor.

The work had gone well from the start. He had started out on the right foot. After blocking out in outline the central position of Nahkla's head, he had drawn beneath it in quite tight outline the naked, well-developed torso of a muscular man. Thus, he trusted, when it came to clothing this upper body in shirt and jacket, he would be able to convey the physical energy latent in the not quite relaxed pose.

So too with the head and features. Nahkla had a very short neck. Not at all languid, his very spherical head seemed planted on his shoulders with the same obstinate, impatient determination to be detected in his eyes. Those eyes were no more than a soft, chestnut brown. But they were framed top and bottom, and encircled about, by pronounced orbital bones. It was the enhanced definition these bones gave the eyes that made them seem extra-human or, at any rate, possessed by someone intent on dominating any dialogue. Once again, even in repose, Nahkla's expression suggested energy on the verge of becoming kinetic.

And Ethan knew he had been lucky! In his first, uninhibited stab at delineating those sockets he had, he saw, captured exactly what he was after, what, in fact, they were. The geometry was everything. The pupils, the irises, the neatly trimmed eyebrows would be a doddle. Forget The Ancient Mariner. Those eyes would rivet the viewer to the spot. Despite the magnificent teeth, he would reject his initial idea of showing Nahkla smiling. The man did not, after all, smile so very much, so very genuinely, in real life. Instead he would paint him with his lips very slightly parted: the expression of a man about to come out with some significant interruption or even spring suddenly to his feet.

Mixing his paints to match Nahkla's complexion was a pleasure. Imagining the light to be coming full and flat from behind the viewer he began to model the features. And now his initial fluency was given pause. He found himself tightening and becoming self-conscious. He was in a unique situation. He was one-on-one with a man he had good reason to believe was a murderer. What cocktail of ego, pride, honour, sensed insult, vindictiveness, bloody mindedness and obsession lay behind these features that he was patiently assembling? Nahkla patently believed he had been disrespected. It was enough to make your hand shake. He found he could only progress by concentrating on the technical details within the square inch or so of the canvas directly under his brush. As the minutes ticked away, as the brush flicked to and fro inches from his own nose, he discovered himself increasingly wondering if he were rendering the image of a distinctive individual or the unwitting depiction of distinct evil. For himself, he began to think, the larger picture might not bear looking at.

Nevertheless, despite his moments of doubt and misgiving, he had undeniably broken the back of his project. He had taken the mandatory look at his work from thirty paces away and had seen that, good likeness though it was, it was a lot more expressive than that alone. As he walked home this late Friday afternoon a distinct mood of relief and accomplishment came pleasurably over him. Until he had feedback from Nahkla, he could relax, proceed through the next few days on cruise control.

Ginny was not back from work when he let himself in. Seeking to draw a line under this first phase of his commission, he dialled the number he had been privileged to have been given for the Waterside Tower penthouse. It rang for a long time, then, just when he thought it would not be answered at all, somebody picked up at the far end.

'Yes? Hello?'

'Er ... this is Ethan Shaw trying to reach Khalid Nahkla.'

'I'm afraid Mr Nahkla is out of the country at present. May I be of any help? I'm Mr Nahkla's personal secretary.'

Again the cut-glass enunciation.

'I hope so. I'm the artist currently executing a portrait of Mr Nahkla.'

'Of course. Mr Shaw. You visited us a few weeks ago.'

'Correct.'

Butter wouldn't melt in that man's mouth any more than blood would stain his immaculate linen.

'The portrait has reached a stage where I need his approval – or otherwise – to carry it on to completion.'

'I understand. I am sure Mr Nahkla is most anxious to view it for himself. He will be in England for a week or so as of next Wednesday. What I can do is e-mail him in Riyadh and try to arrange an appointment for the end of next week. Would that suit?'

'Perfectly.'

'You would come here again?'

'Of course.'

'With the painting?'

'Naturally.'

'Mid-morning?'

'Yes, ideal.'

'Very well. I'll endeavour to set that up. Let me have your e-mail address and I'll get back to you.'

With mild, silent reservations – but he was calling on his mobile – Ethan relayed his details down the line.

'Very good,' Ali said. 'I'll get back to you as soon as.'

They said their goodbyes. What could have been more civilised?

Ali had been as good as his civilised word. Courtesy of e-mail he had seamlessly arranged the date and time for Ethan's second visit to the Waterside Tower. For this occasion, burdened by the unwieldly bulk of his canvas and buoyed by his sense of fresh money in the bank, he had opted to arrive by old fashioned black taxi cab. It would bestow matter-of-fact anonymity upon him at the checkpoint.

'Please state your name and purpose in visiting,' the warrant officer's voice intoned.

'Ethan Shaw to see Mr Khalid Nahkla,' he tried to reply in kind.

'Nature of call?'

'Private.'

The barrier-pole rose anyway. Because he only had one pair of hands, and both the canvas and his satchel to contend, with he paid off his driver while still inside the cab. He was glad of the automatic door system when he sidled into the seemingly restrained vestibule. The concierge, same blazer, same brass buttons, same lazer-straight parting in his short back and sides hair, might not have been away from behind the desk during the weeks that had elapsed since the previous visit. As there was now no manner in which he could be obstructive, he attempted to be dismissive.

'Take the small lift on the left,' he ordered as he reached for his phone.

The lift door slid open. Ethan edged awkwardly inside. Once again the floor vibrated under his feet. Once again he was glided aloft and once again, the further lift door sliding open, found himself confronting, and being confronted by, Ali.

'Allow me,' Ali said pleasantly and with marked deftness had relieved him of the bubble-wrapped canvas. This morning he was wearing the clone, save for its Air Force blue colour, of his tan linen suit. Eyebrows raised enquiringly, Ethan proffered the satchel towards him. Ali shook his head.

'Hardly necessary today,' he said.

Without feeling he need say anything else, he led the way down the short corridor and on into the daylight-saturated extended living room. Ethan had been prepared this time for the dramatic rise in light value as he entered the space, and, his eyes cast down, saw Khalid Nahkla in more than silhouette as he rose from an armchair at the distant end of the room and, hand extended, smiling, coming rapidly forward.

'Greetings. Good morning,' he said.

'Good morning.'

They had shaken hands. Once again it had been a brisk, everyday clasp with no apparent attempt to establish macho superiority or employ any sleight of finger to signal international brotherhood.

'Thank you for being right on time,' Nahkla said. 'I have to confess I'm quite excited about what you've brought with you. Coffee?'

'Er ... Perhaps not just this second. Better to keep coffee and painting well apart perhaps.'

'Ah, of course. Shall we, then? Ali.'

There was a low but four-square armchair close to where they stood. Nahkla had designated this with a quick, nodding glance. Ali carried the bundled up canvas over to it.

'Which way round?' he asked.

'Just as you have it.'

Ali settled the canvas on the horizontal arms of the chair and angled it back against the upholstered back. Taking care to position himself between his handiwork and his client,

Ethan stepped forward to join Ali. Together, patiently, they divested the canvas of all its wrappings. Only now did Ethan allow Nahkla his first clear sight of the work.

'Ah ... ' said Nahkla softly, letting out his breath. 'Ah ... Yes, I like it. I like it a lot, I think. I wouldn't say it's flattering but no doubt it's all the better for that. Yes, I don't think I object at all being remembered like that. It's somehow tight and loose at the same time. It certainly doesn't put me in mind of over-cooked venison at the Christ Church high table.'

'I haven't done the background books yet, obviously.'

'No, no. They can clearly be done anytime.'

'I'm so glad your first impression – '

'Hey, hey! What's that?!'

So he had risen to the bait.

'What's what?'

'That fleck of colour on the tie. The yellow.'

'Gold. It's a tie-pin.'

'A what?!'

'A tie-pin.'

'Good God, man! I haven't worn a tie-pin since I was ten years old! No gentleman wears a tie-pin.'

'Well – '

'It's bling! Nothing but bling! Vulgar! I don't like it. I don't want it. It isn't me.'

That latent energy, ferocity, which Ethan had long since detected in Khalid Nahkla was now no more than millimetres beneath the surface of his skin. He was staring at his portrayer with a displeasure mounting towards an undisguised, appearance-altering fury. Blood had storm-trooped into his face turning the golden tan to thunder-cloud leaden. The skin about his mouth was drawn tightly back up into his rigid cheeks and the splendid teeth were more akin to fangs than seemed humanly possible. The eyes that stared softly brown from the canvas had in the living man become concentrated into small black bullets pregnant with death and destruction. Well, if you played with fire you must expect to be burned.

'I merely – '

'What is it, anyway? What's the device?'

Ethan had been waiting for this moment the entire morning. But he had not expected it to find him so unfounded as this.

'It's a scimitar,' he said.

Khalid Nahkla positively recoiled. He took a clear step backwards and drew himself up to his full straight-shouldered height. Beyond belief, his fury of seconds ago seemed to have intensified. If he gave forth a sound now it would be a hiss.

'And just what possessed you so that you wished that upon me?' he said.

He had not hissed but the words had come thick and muffled as if they had had to fight their way through the blood in his throat.

'I thought it might be emblematic of your heritage,' Ethan said. 'Your culture. Perhaps even your character.'

'And did you so presume?' Nahkla went on. The complexion that had grown so threateningly dark was lightening again now, the voice lightening in tone.

'When have you ever seen me stooping to wearing a tie-pin?' he said, now seemingly regaining control.

'Never. But I – '

'Good God! Didn't I warn you about representing me as a cut rate Omar Sharif? You could just as well have portrayed me with a hawk on my wrist or a tea towel over my head! Didn't it occur to you that you should consult with me about this first?'

'It did, yes,' Ethan risked, 'but you were abroad at the time. I'd had the idea and I thought I'd try it on for size. This is only – '

'It was impertinent of you,' Nahkla said. 'Impertinent and insolent. Worse, it was arguably audacious.'

He was staring piercingly now rather than glaring. Ethan had to strain every psychic nerve to hold that gaze and appear to remain cool under fire.

'Foolhardy, even,' Nahkla added.

'I accept a scimitar tie-pin is inappropriate and probably on several levels not acceptable. But it's no big thing. I can paint it out easily enough, redo the tie.'

Now it was time for him to square his own shoulders.

'Nobody will ever know it was there,' he said. 'It can just be our little secret.'

He held still, forcing himself not to blink, and almost stupefied, realised that for the first time in their acquaintanceship, Nahkla was at a loss for words. It was a double first. Never before had he spoken to an acknowledged heavy-hitter in code.'

'Yes, please do that,' Nahkla said. 'Otherwise, yes ... good. I believe not spoiling the ship for a ha'porth of tar is an English proverb or expression. I'll be back in the UK in fourteen or fifteen days' time. I'll thank you to show me the revised version then.'

Nahkla had turned abruptly on his heel and was stalking to the far end of the room. His knees weak, his throat parched, Ethan realised that he had never before thirsted so badly for a good cup of coffee and that at a time when coffee of any quality, any beverage at all, was most definitely denied him.

He moved to the bubble-wrap and began trying to make sense of its slithery lengths. Ali came to help him.

'I'll call you a taxi,' he said.

Ali carried the re-wrapped portrait back to the penthouse lift. As the lift door slid open he looked at Ethan with a slight smile.

'Oops,' he said.

13

THAT THERE HAD BEEN AN UNMISTAKABLE over-reaction to the red rag, that, regardless of his own safety, he had impulsively flaunted it under Nahkla's nose, was beyond question. But as he knew and as DI Carter had confirmed when he gave her a blow by blow account of the encounter, their dialogue hadn't proved a thing. It only served to strengthen a suspicion as near total as made no difference: as Bradley would have put it, it didn't provide an iota of tangible evidence let alone proof.

'Watch your back,' she had inevitably rung off with.

And, of course, on an immediate, an aesthetic, level Nahkla had been utterly justified in his outburst – the scimitar tie-pin was indeed a grievous artistic miscalculation. Set aside its latent accusation and it was truly nothing but bling. Nahkla was in no way a middle-class soul dressing up flash in an effort to impress his next-door neighbour; whatever pitiless sense of self ran in his alien veins, the man had class and style. He had had the right to blow his top. The splash of gold had been a page one error. Not only did it rob Nahkla of the respect he felt his due, it gave the portrait a false secondary focal point that detracted from the primary intent. A hostile critic could take one look at the painting as it stood and talk of dropped egg yolk.

As the day wore on, by the time that evening, he was telling Ginny what had transpired, it was the dereliction of artistic discernment that rankled most at the back of his mind. In its foreground too. He was like a man who had just put a scratch on his new car. He had failed to keep his eye on the ball that counted. In his eagerness to rattle Nahkla's cage he had been schoolboyishly unprofessional.

Ginny had listened to his story without a word of interruption.

'You'd better put it right, then,' she said at last. 'And, please God, watch your back.'

The following morning, anxious to get on with it, he did set about putting it right. It took longer than he had imagined it would. He would re-order the tie entirely, knot and all. As he erased all hint of gold, slightly reconfigured the hang of the new version tie, it was impossible not to think of Kenneth Marsh honestly cleaning the mediocre, dishonestly confecting the charming. Finally he had it done to his satisfaction. Only he would ever know it, but the truth was that the tie hung better now – there in natural situ but pictorially leading the eye to the features instead of distracting from them. After that painting in the background of suggest book-lined shelves. Finally, the portait complete, he closed the big door to the unit, tired but satisfied.

When he got back to the house, he found Ginny had returned before him. She was sitting in the main room behind a tall gin and tonic.

'I thought we might eat out tonight,' she said.

'Too tired to cook?' he asked.

'In a word, yes.'

'I'll help you. We can do it together.'

'There's something I have to say.'

'We can talk in the kitchen.'

'This is important. I think I'd find it easier to get into it somewhere impersonal. A bit formal.'

He felt his gut grow hollow and chill on him. This could only be one thing. He'd quite forgotten the portrait now. What would life be like without Ginny?

'I already called La Bella Vista,' Ginny said. 'I just managed to book a table. If we go now, we've got just a quarter of an hour.'

'I need to tidy up,' he said.

They had proved on numerous occasions that the front door to La Bella Vista was no more than five minutes' walk but thinking the unthinkable – trying hard not to think the unthinkable – he had never covered the distance with such leaden steps. All too soon, somehow, they had arrived. He opened the restaurant's door and stepped aside. The place was packed and busy.

By chance, Giorgio, their favourite waiter, was serving at a table close to the entrance. He saw them at once and nodded his greeting. Replacing a bottle of white in its bucket he led them directly to a table for two towards the restaurant's rear. With a sickening sense of life's not so little ironies, Ethan recognised this was the exact table over which not so very long ago in the past he and Ginny had met and, as he had supposed, began to fall in love.

Giorgio pulled back one chair for Ginny.

'To drink?' he asked as they sat.

'We'll go straight to the wine, please, Giorgio,' Ginny said. 'A bottle of the house white.'

'And I'll also have a glass of the red,' Ethan said. Even at this point he could still think ahead on one level.

'Very good,' Giorgio said, and was gone.

'Well?' Ethan said across the table.

Ginny looked at him, sat up straight and breathed out a breath. His stomach seemed to tense of its own accord as he held his own breath.

'I've had a letter,' Ginny said.

'Yes?'

'From Imogen.'

'From ... '

'My niece. My older niece.'

Suddenly Ginny had gulped and with total surprise he realised that she was straining every nerve not to break down and cry.

'It's heartbreaking,' she got out.

He reached across the table and caught hold of her wrist.

'Easy now,' he said. 'Easy.'

She was silent. Her eyes were watering but not yet weeping. She swallowed, brought her head up, had regained some sort of control.

'I think she must have smuggled it out,' she said. 'The envelope's all wrong for the paper and it's all smudged as if she was crying. The spelling's atrocious.'

'You have it with you?'

She shook her head.

'No. I was too ashamed to bring it. Oh, Ethan, it's all my fault! I've neglected them so badly. I've just not taken proper care of them.'

He squeezed her hand as hard as he thought she could bear. It was amazing – improper – how someone else's misery should trigger such a gush of relief flooding anyone with happiness.

'But you write to them every week,' he said, 'and you send them all those postcards. And the food parcel treats.'

'It's not enough!' she cried. 'I've been nothing but selfish. I haven't visited them in months.'

'Probably on my account.'

'Well ... yes. But I should have known better. I did know better. Ethan – they're orphans! They're only nine and seven and I'm their godmother. Imogen says how lonely they are.'

'What about that Mrs – their "nanny" – '

'Connors. I think she's the other villain in the piece. She was supposed to visit them every weekend – she's paid to, God damnit! – but Imogen says she only comes for short visits and doesn't take them out anywhere and hasn't come at all the last two weeks. I fancy she's found herself some bloke who can't be bothered with waifs and strays.'

'Well ... '

'Ethan, I'm going down there. To Taunton. I'm going to stop at a hotel for a couple of days and then stay with Valerie Hargreaves, my old school friend. I'll see them – Imogen and Cordelia – take them out, talk to them. Imogen says the other girls laugh at them because they've got no mummy and daddy.'

'There's no-one more vicious than school-kids.'

'Ethan – I think I want to adopt them.'

'Well ... '

'I've been to see lawyers – serious grown-up ones. London. Chancery Lane. It wouldn't be easy. I'm their nearest blood relative, their aunt, and, like I said, their godparent, but I'm also a single female who may be white but is also essentially broke.'

Giorgio suddenly returned with a bottle of Pinot Grigio and an ice bucket. He looked enquiringly at them in turn.

'Just pour, please,' Ginny gulped out.

Giorgio did just that. Ginny had snatched her glass up before he had reached forward towards Ethan's.

'The red is for the main course, yes?' he asked Ethan.

'Yes.'

'Fegato, yes?'

'Indeed.'

'And to start, bruschetta?'

'Naturally.'

'And for you, signorina, your main course?'

'Er ... I think I'll just have the Salad Caprese.'

'As a mains, yes, very good.'

He was gone. Ethan looked across the table at Virginia.

'So this is what you wanted to talk about?' he said.

She grabbed at her glass again and took a huge slurp of wine that she could not possibly have savoured.

'Not only that,' she said. 'Not that entirely ... '

Now it was she who was looking at him.

'Ethan,' she said, 'not so very long ago we were talking and somehow we ended up sort of mutually proposing to each other and we agreed to get married.'

'Vowed even,' he said. 'We did. And we will.'

'But can we do it right away – as soon as possible?'

'Why?'

'Oh it's not just because it will be such a convenience in applying to adopt. It's because I need and want you, love you so much. Please, please, please – marry me tomorrow.'

As had happened originally he was lost for words again. What do you say when hard on the heels of cruellest despair your world and happiness are made complete?

'It's not a Leap Year,' some fool remarked.

'Oh sod that for a game of silly buggers,' she came out with as her eyes grew wider than he had ever known.

'More than ever I will be honoured to,' he said.

Her eyelids closed. Again she blew out breath. Her shoulders eased forward as she lost her tenseness.

'Oh bless you, my love,' she said.

'How could I not?' he said.

She raised his left hand to her mouth and kissed it. There was still a trace of burnt-umber on the ring finger's knuckle.

'For the past couple of months,' he said, 'I've been churning over in my mind whether or not I should ask you that same question. "When?" I think there are two reasons why I didn't.'

'Two?'

'Yes. The first, the important one, is that every morning I've woken up, I've asked myself what could be better between you and me than what we've got now. And not being married, in a way, makes each day more special, if you know what I mean, another special commitment rather than the blank cheque of a marriage licence. Does that make sense?'

'Perfect sense.'

'The second reason – not exactly a negligible one now in view of what you've just told me – is that however broke you are I'm broker still. When it comes to worldly goods, you for the endowing with, I'm not likely to appear much of a catch in the view of some child welfare jobsworth.'

'But who else could I begin to think of marrying? Anyway, I don't think they're all jobsworths.'

Later when Giorgio had come and gone again and they were midway through the meal Ginny laid her fork aside for a moment.

'It'll have to be a registry office,' she said.

'Yes. I'll get on to the town hall first thing tomorrow. It won't be a stylish marriage.'

'But legal and binding. Do you think you'll be able to cope with taking on board two semi-grown up human beings as you embark on matrimony?'

'Well, as you are wont to say, there's only one way to find out. It's not so much a tandem we'll need as a bicycle made for four.'

For the first time that evening he saw her, all strain gone now, smile.

'Of course a ring or two won't come amiss now, will they? And you'll never guess what kind of an engagement present I'm going to be giving you.'

The idea had come to him. He took out his mobile to record the setting.

'Is this Mr Shaw?' Ali asked down the line.

'Speaking,' Ethan replied.

'I've just fielded your message. How may I be of help?'

'I've completed the ... er ... modification to Mr Nahkla's portrait and was hoping to arrange a further viewing with him.'

'Ah yes. The make-over. I'm sorry to tell you, Mr Shaw, but, as is so often the case, Mr Nahkla is not in the country at present.'

'Ah. When is he expected back?'

'Several days hence, at least. He hasn't yet let us know.'

'I wonder in that case if it would be possible to drop the portrait off with you to await his return?'

'Perfectly possible, I'm sure. When would you like to bring it along?'

'How about right now?'

'Yes certainly, that will be no problem. I shall be here all morning.'

Within thirty minutes, the taxi having fully negotiated the check-point interrogation, Ethan again stood one on one before the Waterside Tower's concierge.

'Mr Nahkla's not here today,' the old soldier said with clerkly satisfaction. He was the type, Ethan sourly realised, who would have worn a pin in his regimental tie if he'd had the wit to think doing so would increase his perceived status in the eyes of his neighbours and inferiors.

'So I understand,' Ethan said. 'But I am only here to deliver this package to his apartment.'

'Big enough for a package ain' – er – isn't it?' the concierge said. 'Right. You can leave it here with me. I'll see to – '

'Mr Nahkla expressly instructed me to deliver it in person. To hand it over to one of his staff, that is. I wouldn't want to – '

'All right. All right,' the concierge said flatly, reaching for his phone. He looked up peevishly from bloodshot eyes, as for the sake of his Christmas bonus he made compliance his priority.

'Be down in two minutes,' he said as he replaced the phone.

Ali made it in a longer-seeming minute and half. It was the tan suit this time – spiccer and spanner than ever.

He flicked his brown, lustrous eyes in a downward glance at the newly bubble-wrapped canvas. He really was most outrageously, rakishly, handsome.

'Tie-pin gone?' he said.

'What tie-pin?' Ethan replied.

His teeth were too good to be true as well.

14

GINNY HAD GONE OFF TWO DAYS ago. He had driven her rather needlessly – she had only taken one smallish grip – to Paddington and they had said a dry-eyed goodbye there. Over the immediately preceding weekend she had been quiet and reflective, not her usual caustic surface-self at all. But the setting out seemed to have revived her: the mere mechanics of organising her trip had returned to her a sense of determined purpose.

When he returned to the house it seemed as silent as a tomb and to have grown five times bigger than he remembered. He spent the rest of the day and part of the next morning doing household chores. When he found himself inventing new ones just for the sake of passing time, he reminded himself that since the devil made work for idle hands, it would be as well to make some for himself. OK then. Get on with it.

That afternoon he travelled halfway across London to visit the discount Art Supplies centre in Whitechapel which he had made use of in his student days. There, along with replenishing some of his basic colours, he bought three canvases, one large, two small. That evening staying on until fairly late in his work unit studio and the waning daylight no issue, he primed all three. He went up to his lonely bed quite early and tired.

There was only one engagement-wedding gift he could present Ginny with and it seemed so obvious as to be corny. But portraits were what he did. If he could pull this one off – do her that justice – it would be a gift, a marker, to treasure for life, whatever course the future years might set them on. It would commemorate a momentous watershed moment in their lives. And in a uniquely personal way. But would the reach of his technique be able to match the grasp of his imagination? A dozen times in the past he had thought of painting her. Only to shrink from the idea. She was so subtly various, so ... fine. He knew her so well he would never be able to render her adequately. Except ... now he thought he might have a way. He wouldn't paint a formal portrait at all. He would paint her loosely, sitting at a restaurant table across from the lucky beholder, her temporary companion. He would paint the *nowness*, the quiddity of the moment. If he concentrated on the fundamental specifics of the scene – the cutlery, the half-filled wine glasses – Ginny's inner beauty and grace might shine through as it always did eventually in life. Hell, the painting would be for them anyway; not for some toffee-nosed academic.

He had the dynamics of the composition, the artless pose, the angling of the table-top sketched out in his mind in full detail. Nevertheless, the next morning, sitting at his easel in the well-lit opening to his work-unit, he set about charcoaling on to the canvas the key co-ordinates of what he envisaged. He would cheat slightly on the viewpoint. Part of it would be at the viewer's sitting eye-level; part, the table top, from a slightly higher angle. Not that you'd get to notice.

He was busy puzzling through the geometrical problems

the composition gave him when, not really registering it, he heard the slick swish of car tyres on the asphalt outside and from the corner of his eye saw something shiny and bright glide otherwise silently into the parking bay of the adjacent unit. As far as he knew nobody had yet rented that one. Nobody had ever come there. Well, the vehicle was out of sight now, let it also be out – he heard a car door open and then thunk shut. In a second the sounds were repeated. Then nothing. No further noises, no foot-falls. He returned to the problem of the tablecloth.

The light on his canvas had deteriorated, darkened. Yes, now he heard a scrape of shoe-leather. He looked up in annoyance. Two men, more silhouetted than not, were walking to his own unit from either side of the wide, commercial entrance. Both men had guns in their hands. Before he had visually identified them he knew them to be Ali and Abu. He knew too that in no way were they to be snidely patronised as 'Alice in Wonderland' odd balls. Most of all he knew that, in spite of repeated warnings, he had failed to watch his back.

Abu, to his left, said something in Arabic.

'Mr Nahkla would like to see you,' Ali said.

Guns. In broad daylight. Not what you expected at the outer end of the Goldhawk Road. He felt otherworldly disbelief and his knees weaken as his stomach turned mushy. But he shouldn't let on.

'I understood Mr Nahkla to be abroad at present,' he said to Ali. 'You told me so yourself.'

'He came back,' Ali said. 'He's waiting.'

'I'd have appreciated a little more in the way of an advanced notice,' Ethan said. 'As you can possibly make out, I'm rather pre-occupied right now.'

'This won't take long,' Ali said.

There was a grating noise. Metal on metal. Ethan turned in the direction of the sound. Stone-faced, unperturbed Abu was screwing a silencer home into the nozzle of the automatic he was carrying. The gun in Ali's hand, however, remained unwaveringly horizontal. As steady as a rock. Ethan felt a tremor of chill fear pass downwards, from a brain that now believed only too well, into all his vitals. It was that same tremor of fear anticipating imminent and unavoidable peril he had three times known in Belfast. He laid down the stick of charcoal he found he had been holding all this while on the lip of his easel.

'To hear is to obey,' he said.

'Very wise,' Ali murmured.

Ali said something else in Arabic as Ethan walked towards them. They were suddenly very close to him, crowding him on either side. The air was heavy with the scent of patchouli.

'I would like to close the door,' he managed to get out quite evenly. 'There's a masterpiece in there.'

Ali lightly laughed.

'By whom?' he asked. 'Please, go ahead.'

They pressed even more tightly to him as he reached up and swung the counter-balanced door down. They were carrying their guns, he was feelingly aware, pressed close to their outer thighs and with the barrels pointing down. No, he wouldn't stand a chance.

'This way, if you would,' Ali said, motioning with his gun-free hand.

The car was a Lexus saloon. Biggish. He neither knew nor cared to know what model it was. But as they shepherded him around its rear end, he did clock and memorise the licence plate. Perhaps ...

'Take the front seat, please,' Ali said, the gun now hard against his ribs.

He duly took the front passenger seat. As he did so, Abu had slid into the rear seat behind him, while Ali closed the passenger front door and continued on around the front of the car en route to the driving seat. The Lexus had that new car smell. Ethan was unthinkingly watching Ali slide his long body down behind the steering wheel when something flesh-creepingly snake-like brushed his hair and slithered around his neck. Something bit unpleasantly into the flesh just below his Adam's apple.

'Heavy gauge fishing line,' Ali said. 'Don't struggle and it won't get any tighter.'

He set the car into smooth forward motion. It swung round in a complacently arrogant arc across the industrial estate's broad general courtyard, glided easily along the private approach lane and then turned right and southwards out on to the public roadway proper. Inside a minute and a half it was passing within fifty yards of where he and Ginny ... He and Ginny. His heart, mind and stomach all clenched as one. His brain felt waterlogged. No! He must not groan out loud. But he had every ground for doing so. Fool! He had missed his chance. Before, outside, however dire the odds against, he had missed his chance. At whatever cost he might have damaged one of them; might have caused enough commotion to leave traces, evidence, a smoking gun. But now – nothing. No chance left. It was part of the pattern, wasn't it? When they played rough – for keeps – Nahkla was always out of the country.

The car was working its way eastwards now on the Hammersmith one-way system. Trying desperately to force his stalled brain out of its abject surrender, he sat reconsidering the odds. The two of them must be about his age. They both had two or three inches in height over him but he had the chunkier, more muscular build. He'd always more than held his own in army unarmed combat sessions. But that had been four years or more in the past. He'd had no reason to stay hard since. They, on the other hand, whatever border skirmishes they had cut their teeth on, no doubt still had every reason to keep themselves in tip-top shape. They probably worked out, day in, day out, at some extortionately charging Knightsbridge gym. And they had guns. He didn't even have his Stanley knife.

What to do? What to do? What to do? They were approaching the big Hammersmith traffic hub now. He realised that he had been sitting in the plush leather seat staring out through the windscreen glass at the mundane swirl of traffic and people and taking absolutely nothing in. But look! There was a police car parked outside the tube entrance and, yes, another whisking around that corner! Forget it. For all the good they could do him, they might as well have been on the moon. Making him feel close to gagging, Abu's fingers were feelingly on the garotte thing around his throat. His seat-belt, somehow, was tight around and across him. What was there he *could* do? Not dive out the door; not wrench the steering wheel to crash-causing side. The first victim, first fatality would be himself.

Again he despaired. Fate had dealt him a pretty rubbishy set of cards – his art skills apart – when he'd been born. But down the years he hadn't played them too badly, all things considered. But what a mother and father of all bummers it was that just when everything had gelled at last and, meeting Ginny he had found purpose and point in his life and, yes, love and every reason to go on living – Christ! He wouldn't go down without a fight! God. They'd know they'd been in one!

Ali was driving crossing Hammersmith Bridge now. To the left, several bends of the Thames downstream, was the Waterside Tower. Not going there, presumably. No. Straight on down Castelnau Road, past The Red Lion and so as well the Wild Fowl place, bearing left slightly with the traffic thinning out and the road narrowing. Yes, Barnes Common up ahead and, as a humpbacked bridge tested the Lexus's suspension so that the loop around his already self-conscious throat jerked painfully tighter, there it was off to the left – not really a common any more but a handful of sports pitches lightly fringed by trees that hardly added up to woodland status. Not more than clumps of copse, you'd have to say.

Ali said something in Arabic again to Abu. He felt the garotte twitch as Abu moved about behind him. Ali had his eyes on the rear-view mirror. Abu said something brief and to some point. Abruptly Ali had violently circled the steering wheel hard left. The car side-stepped like a startled horse. Its chassis juddered on a stem to stern diagonal as it left the metalled road, mounted and scalped a stretch of verge, came back down literally to earth. It was travelling now at a good twenty-five along the parallel dirt lines worn into the grass by the toing and froing of whatever vehicles the maintenance teams brought to the common. There continued to be short, sharp shocks to the suspension system. Each one served to remind Ethan of the oily tightness chafing at his neck. The noisome irritation seemed as much inside his throat as out. No! He would not retch.

Ali was braking, clearly searching the ragged hedgerow to his right. He was turning that way. Now the car was progressing slowly down a lesser track along an unbrokenly green surface.

Leaves, twists of bramble, slapped steadily at either side with an angry loudness.

Then quiet. The engine hum now audible, the car was entered upon an unexpected small space, too small to be called a glade. Here, sliding sideways a little as Ali finally braked, the car came to a halt.

'Out, if you please,' Ali said.

For long seconds Ethan thought not to obey. If this was the end of the line, he would make them do it the hard and messy way. But how logical was that? Outside of the car, on his feet, he might still be able to throw one good punch, dive at a knee, go down fighting. Sitting, he was a dead duck twice over. The noose jerked his head back and decided him. He clicked free from his safety-belt and, allowed to do so, edged out of the car.

As he rose to his feet he snatched a glance behind. Not a trace of another vehicle, another human being. The car, of course, was coloured a mid-green. He straightened up and looked ahead. Yet another shock-wave jolted through his solar plexus. Across the clearing, propped against a thin tree, stood a couple of common or garden spades. Beside them was an untidy heap of dark subsoil and a stack of shaggily irregular grass turves. Forward of these piles was a long, pitch-dark scar upon the surface of the ground. Ali motioned in that direction with his gun.

'Over there. Please,' he said. Quite casually too.

Ethan weighed his chances. Zilch. It was fifteen yards to the further trees. From a standing start he had no prospect of out-running, out-swerving their fire. The trees beyond were too thin and too thinly spaced to offer cover. If he was going to make a fight of it, this was the spot.

But they were keeping their distance. He would need to

take two strides before he could throw that one puny punch. No way. He straightened his shoulders. He'd be damned if he'd let them think he'd lost his nerve and bolted. All right. Bring it on.

Making sure that he walked very steadily he set off across the clearing. So near and now so far! Ginny! He'd never get to paint her portrait now. But she knew of his intention. It was the thought that would have to be her souvenir. She would survive. She was brave, resourceful, brainy. She would have a life. And while he would never have the privilege of observing it, through Ginny, so too would her nieces.

He came to a natural halt. The scar upon the ground was a narrow trench about six feet long and some two feet deep. Rest in Peace.

'You've worked hard,' he heard himself say, 'but not hard enough. The foxes will be into that in nothing flat.'

'That won't be any great concern of yours,' Ali said. 'Kneel down, please.'

'Go piss up a rope,' Ethan said.

Something in Ali's face softened rather than hardened at this outburst. He said something swift in Arabic.

The pressure about Ethan's neck was suddenly reduced. Even as he felt this beginning to happen, a hand pulled his forehead backwards. Scrabbling, muffling, blinding, darkness was upon him, stifling him for breath. A gun barrel pressed hard against the nape of his neck. Penrith, he thought with added panic-induced horror, his head in that black bag. Bracing his shoulders he pushed back hard against the gun.

'No way!' he shouted. 'If you're going to do it, do it looking me straight in the eyes, you fucking murderous jackals.'

The pressure of the gun was gone. Fingers thickly groped at his scalp. Startling him, jerking his head violently back again, the cloth was pulled roughly off his head. Daylight blindingly rescued him from the loathsome claustrophobia and, more startlingly still, standing facing him a yard away, suavely dressed, in a drab olive safari suit, and holding a black cloth, was Khalid Nahkla.

'Mr Shaw,' Nahkla said.

There was nothing to say to that. He sucked in air and, nothing but disorientated, wondered if his disbelief was evaporating or increasing.

'That, I can inform you,' Nahkla went on, 'is as far as today's exercise will proceed. You may be thoroughly assured that you are in no danger now. I give you my word.'

Nahkla said something in fast, fluent Arabic in which, possibly, the name Ibrahin might have featured. Abu-Ibrahin, therefore, stepped forward into plain sight for the first time in perhaps twenty minutes. In his hand he carried a flat length of gleaming metal. His long slender thumb clicked something and the knife doubled in length as its blade shot forward into view. Abu-Ibrahin's golden-olive features loomed abruptly into a still blinking-impeded close-up as, garlic on his breath qualifying the patchouli, he delicately, even gently, slipped the tip of the knife-blade between the nylon noose and the flesh it ringed. Ethan felt a smooth coolness and then with a distinct 'ping' the constriction was vanished away. He swivelled his neck from side to side for the sheer pleasure of it.

'You are an intelligent man,' Nahkla now chose to continue. 'The point of the exercise will not be lost on you. It has been to drive home how easily you may be found, reached and expertly dealt with, should you ever again choose to make a nuisance of yourself.'

'I thought that I'd already made it quite clear,' Ethan said, his voice thick, his throat raw, 'that unless you gave further cause, I had absolutely no intention of bothering you further. You had my own word on that.'

Nahkla looked those pointed, blackened pupils at him as his mouth pursed and his hissed-out breath seemed to tighten his face.

'More impertinence,' he said. 'What credit in the world do you think your puny word commands? You may consider today as a case of being better safe than sorry. As, narrowly you find your own self.'

He handed the black bag to Ali, who, a gun no longer in his hand, was now at his side.

Ethan gestured towards the trench.

'This would have been sloppy if you'd gone through with it,' he said. 'Tyre tracks, scratched car body, an impossibly shallow grave, forensics would have been on to you in no time. Not to mention my known connection to Penrith.'

'There are ways for some of making forensics irrelevant,' Nahkla said with apparent seriousness. 'But, as I have just made clear, there never was any intention of going ahead with what you were led to expect. It was a means of making a point emphatically.'

'Let me concede,' Ethan replied, 'that if your point was to scare me shitless, you may consider it well and truly made. Meanwhile let me remind you that in this country kidnapping is a crime.'

Nahkla allowed himself to expend another of his meagre supply of smiles.

'You will do very well to remain permanently scared,' he said. 'As to possible prosecution – on any charge – I do have, how shall I put it ... a certain number of in-depth contacts, allies, so to call them, very familiar with the mechanics of various institutions and with the levers of decision making within those organisations. All in all I can have recourse to the best defensive measures imaginable.'

'Well, there's a surprise.'

'I may say that from some of these sources I have satisfied myself that your coming into contact with Rupert Penrith was entirely coincidental as regards his elaborate attempt to betray his acquaintanceship with me by a squalid and insulting huckster's swindle.'

'Ah, that reminds me. You made one big-time goof in trying to suit his punishment to his crime.'

'Oh?'

'When you were discerning enough to buy my Box Hill landscape, he duly subtracted his immediate commission from the sales-price and wrote me out a cheque for the balance before my own eyes. He was left-handed. Your errand boys here sawed off the wrong pandy. Not, as things turned out, it mattered.'

This time, Nahkla did not smile at all. He did not quite audibly hiss either. Eyes again like gimlets, he glared his stare balefully back at Ethan.

'Affairs of honour and just retribution,' he said, 'are properly treated not literally but figuratively. It is my deepest regret that Penrith did not survive his operation. I would much have preferred that he had lived on to proclaim his shame – his status as a shabby thief – to anyone shrewd enough to put two and two together. Which hand he might better wipe his backside with was never my concern.'

'No, I determined you innocent as not proven guilty. I also admire your talent – you have a spark. I would be sorry to see that spark extinguished – be the cause of its being snuffed out. I would hope we might both live on longer to see further examples of your talent manifesting themselves. Oh, by the way, I have examined your reworking of my portrait. I find it much more to my liking. Splendid, indeed. Very me.'

'Well, thank you for small mercies. I do think I got the bloody-mindedness right.'

Nahkla blinked once and visibly weighed in his mind the words he was going to come out with.

'That's another thing,' he said. 'To use a word that might seem strange to you coming from me, I have to acknowledge that I admire your chutzpah. I sit on the boards of two of the world's most important oil companies. I exert political influence within and between several nation states. I have sat across negotiating tables with various celebrated heads of government – Muammar al-Gaddafi, Benjamin Netanyahu, say. There's no question that on occasion I've been a thorn in the sides of various eminent men. But I don't recall anyone ever coming at me as directly as you presumed to do.'

'Directly? I considered that I had acted covertly, discreetly.'

'It was direct enough from where I was standing. As I could see that you saw at the time.'

'I considered that we had achieved an understanding. "You don't tell, I who have no real evidence, don't tell." But then I'm not used to talking in code. You were quite right about the tie-pin, by the way, of course. I might just as well have presented the painting with egg yolk spilled down its front.'

Nahkla nodded.

'Perhaps in the fullness of time,' he said, 'that will seem the essential issue. Oh, by the way, to deal with an unessential issue – there is no point in you or any interested friends you may have fretting about the fate or even the whereabouts of Penrith's worthless little receptionist. Wondering whether to start searching for her remains, indeed. She is perfectly safe and well. It is a fact that she did lose the one true love of her life a while ago, but provision has been made to obtain her another and she is currently married and gainfully employed in what may be described as a galaxy far, far away. Arrangements have been made, in short, to allow her to rise higher in the world than she could otherwise have expected.'

'How very convenient for one and all,' Ethan said. 'I thought that we had an arrangement – a gentleman's agreement. I didn't expect these juvenile melodramatics.'

Khalid Nahkla stood still, considering. Abu had now come to flank him as well.

'I considered that it was necessary to impress upon you that the divide between chutzpah and insolent impertinence is hairline thin but quite assuredly there,' he said. 'If I've done no more than that I may have rendered you a long-term service. But perhaps to a degree I did misjudge the situation. Perhaps I did over-react. But not previously. You won't deny, I'm sure, that the world has been purged of two vile excrescences.'

'Yes, look on the bright side. I dare say your two goons enjoyed themselves just as much today as they did previously.'

'They merely obey instructions. Perhaps in time I can improve your impression of me.'

'We'll have to see.'

Nahkla gathered himself, looked from left to right.

'We've rather brought you out of your way,' he said. 'Perhaps we can offer you a ride back home.'

'Thanks for the offer,' Ethan said. 'It's a pleasant day. I think I'd rather walk.'

He marched straight forwards, then bent his path to go around them. Ali stuck out his hand and touching his shoulder brought him to a halt.

'You did well,' Ali said. 'Nothing personal.'

'Yes it was,' Ethan said. 'Don't forget your spades.'

It took him nearly all afternoon to walk back. After, plunging into the apology of a wood, he had left them well behind, he found himself quite unstrung. The let-down was total and enormous. His knees, weak and rubbery, were so out of control he could not walk straight. Quivering, he lurched from side to side in real danger of pitching forward on to his face. Tremors were coursing the length and breadth of his body as hot flushes chased each other through his veins. His breath was coming and going with a mind of its own. Was this what they meant when they talked of hyperventilating? Ugh! Involuntarily he had hawked. Thick, acrid, oily bile was flooding the back of his throat. He straightened slightly, tilted his head back, swallowed the muck back down and wiped his flooded eyes dry. He'd be all right if he sat down for a moment. But there was nothing here to sit on. He staggered to a tree trunk and seized it with his left hand. The tremors ran into its solidity and kicked up his arm and shaking on into his chest. He closed his eyes, lowered his head breathed in slowly and deeply. Those bastards! Those slick, smug bastards. If he could just get to kill them! Just once! He thought back to his Service Corps days and recovering from the forced marches. Give it time and you got your equilibrium back again. So too now then ... Gradually his pulse slowed to normal as his temperature dropped and he was breathing naturally. Ten minutes later he could go on.

He quit the artificial country and was trudging the made-up road once more. Passing The Red Lion this second time, he went in and downed two pints of lager in nothing flat. He failed to taste a drop but didn't care: it was the weight of the liquid, the re-hydration that his parched system screamed for. It was amazing. The cheerful young barmaid, the few sparsely spread other afternoon customers, had no idea that there in their midst and before their very eyes was a man who an hour ago had thought himself dead meat and food for foxes.

He ordered a third pint and made himself drink it slowly, being sure to taste every drop so that in the process he might submit himself to a reality check. No, the shakes were gone; he had the disbelieving, the enormity factor, under control now. It had happened. He was out the other side now. There was a logic, however bizarre, as to why it had happened and to why he had emerged. Like a million and one other incidents in his ragged previous, it could now be chalked up to experience and filed away.

He wouldn't call for a taxi. The long walk up Castelnau would be his decompression chamber as he continued to leave the experience behind. When he had crossed the bridge and was into built-up Hammersmith he put twenty minutes on his journey back by ducking into an unprepossessing single-fronted electronics shop. There he bought two identical el cheapo burner mobile phones. The salesman, a lank-haired, bespectacled and pock-marked Asian man had served him with all the laconic indifference of a man well accustomed to dealing with low-level drug pedlars and suburban adulterers. Nevertheless, the transaction was healing. When he came back out on the street again everything looked normal. As much as he was ever going to be, he was himself again.

That evening, not long after he had put both the new phones on charge, the landline rang. It was Ginny calling as pre-arranged.

'How are you making out?' he asked.

'Splendidly,' she answered. 'Everything's coming up roses.

I've seen both the girls and – look, there's a lot to tell you. I'll save it until we're face to face. I'm meeting the headmistress tomorrow. How have things been at your end?'

'Oh, very quiet,' he said.

15

YES, THE DEVIL MADE WORK FOR idle hands. Three mornings after his little excursion into the Barnes Common countryside, Ethan was hard at it completing what he thought of as phase one of the portrait of Virginia Faulkner. Working on her features, he had modelled the face and, after considerable trouble, arrived at the precise shading of her complexion when lit by the artificial lighting of a small restaurant. He had just finished putting in the highlight to one of her eyes when his mobile rang. Talk of the devil, he thought.

'Hello?' he said.

'Ethan Shaw?'

No, not Alec Bradley. A woman.

' ... er ... yes. Speaking.'

'DI Carter.'

'Ah – yes. Hello – sorry, I – '

'You don't remember me, do you?'

'Yes, yes. Very well. It was just that I was expecting a call from someone else. How are you?'

'Ish. A bit discombobulated.'

'Oh? Why's that?'

'I'll explain. Oh, this call's off-line, by the way. Not official, not recorded.'

'Aren't they the best sort?'

'Most interesting, maybe. The thing is I was summoned to New Scotland Yard yesterday. One-on-one with the Commissioner, no less. Unprecedented in the whole seventeen years of my inglorious career.'

'You get a rocket?'

'No. A warning, in effect. Belt and braces time. He confirmed what I already knew – as I told him – namely that the Penrith case was well and truly put to bed, so no further investigations or enquiries to be undertaken.'

'Well, there's a waste of my taxpayer's contributions.'

'They're going to want more for your pound of flesh. He told me a meeting was being set up between me and quote an important senior official from the Home Office unquote.'

'Who's that when he's at home?'

'A low-level spook, I'm willing to bet. I was told the meeting would be highly confidential. Also, off-line. Not to be discussed with anyone.'

'You're discussing it with me.'

'That's the point. The one exception. I've strict unofficial orders to rope you in on it as well.'

'Me?!'

'Your very good self.'

'Why ... ? What if I tell you and your Commissioner to go shove it? Which I'm well inclined to do.'

'There'd be nothing much I or anyone else could do about it. Immediately. I dare say in due course your tax returns might be found a bit wanting and you might well get to hear a lot of strange crackling on your phone line. Plus it wouldn't do much for my promotion prospects – non-existent as they largely are anyway.'

'Well ... '

'It would probably be a lunch. All I'm really offering you is a hot meal. Probably not a very good one.'

'Well, if it helps you personally, OK. And if it's a case of you personally drawing a line under the investigation, I am now in a position to remove any last lingering doubts from your thinking.'

'Meaning what?'

'I'm glad you called. I've been wondering these past couple of days whether or not to call you.'

'To say what?'

As briefly and as matter-of-factly as possible, indeed in his best inquest witness box manner, Ethan told DI Carter about his being taken for a ride. He could hear her listening down the line.

'Jesus Christ!' she said at last. 'You must have been petrified.'

'I was eventually. After they let me go, I damn near fainted. While it was going on I think I must have been in deep shock – not quite believing it was happening, trying to seem cool under pressure. It was the overwhelming relief that nearly did me in.'

'I've been in that place after ... after things.'

'The point I'm making is that when he was being "Mr Nice Guy" for my benefit, it was totally implicit that Nahkla and his boy scouts did for Penrith. He made it clear – the patronising bastard – that I was the most insignificant fly in his ointment. He spoke of having seriously heavy protection – "in depth" was the way he put it – if push should ever come to shove between him and Her Majesty's Judiciary.'

'That will be exactly why I'm getting to meet this gink from Millbank. You don't have to come, you know.'

'No, if it helps you, I'll come. I'll say the right things. When will it be?'

'To be arranged. To suit said gink's pleasure and convenience no doubt. I'll get back to you with the as and the when. How's Virginia?'

'Fine. Looking great. We've decided to get married.'

'Good on you. Every congratulation.'

Needlessly, no doubt, superfluously, to be sure, he had driven up to Paddington a second time so as to meet Ginny on her return from the West Country. She came into his arms on the concourse in a way that told him he would enjoy the evening. When they were at last shut up in the Toyota they could talk properly.

'How'd it go?' he said as they crawled down Praed Street.

'Oh, Ethan! It was terrific! I'm so glad I thought to go.'

'They enjoyed it, then ... ?'

'Absolutely! You could see them coming alive. As I said on the phone they were a little bit dubious at first – uptight – but when the ice was broken and they could tell they truly were released from durance vile, their batteries started to get charged up and never stopped.'

'What did you do?'

'Everything. I arranged to take them to Bath for the weekend. I showed them the baths and told them about the Romans – they'd never had any idea the Romans had been here so long. I showed them the Pump room and talked about Jane Austen; never heard of her, needless to say. There's a historic costumes museum in Bath so I took them to see that and they loved that to bits and ditto the museum full of American patchwork quilts and so on – which you'd have liked too. And – oh, yes – I stood them a, you know, grown-up dinner in my hotel and that really did wonders for their self-esteem and we went to umpteen tea shops and had knickerbocker glories and heaven knows how many – '

'Bath buns?'

'Well, sticky cakes, anyway.'

'It doesn't show on you.'

'I'm not so sure.'

'We'll check later. What about the school?'

'That's another reason I'm so glad I went. The second day, that headmistress, Mrs Lusby, insisted on my taking a grand tour with her. Standard practice with all parents, pretty obviously. Ethan, it was so sterile, so sanitised! All she could go on about was how small the classes were, how specialised. She kept saying how character and deportment were just as important as academic qualifications.

'The building itself is very nice. William and Mary originally, as she kept reminding me – the tennis courts apart. Imogen and Cordelia are a bit young for Jane Austen but I couldn't resist giving them each a copy of *Northanger Abbey* yesterday when I said goodbye to them. I gave them a starter for ten. I told them the story showed that people who seemed very nice to start with could turn out to be quite nasty and that people who seemed nothing much at first could end up being very nice. Ethan, it will soon be their summer holiday. I softened our parting by saying they should come and stay with us in London. That thrilled them.'

'You told them about me?'

'I told them I was going to get married. That really excited them too.'

'It does me too. But it'll be difficult for them to be bridesmaids.'

'Oh, Ethan, we can't leave them down there for their brains to rot. We must get them up here with us – find them a good *working* school.'

'Well, we will.'

'You can teach them to draw.'

'I can show them a few tricks. With drawing, by and large, you've either got it or you haven't. Talking of gifts – if you open the glove compartment, you'll find a little something in there for you.'

'Oh?'

Doing as she was bid, Ginny opened the compartment's flap. Inside, still in their boxes, were the el cheapo burner phones.

'What are these about?' she asked. 'They've got to be surplus to requirements.'

'That female DI, DI Carter, called me the other day,' he began to invent, 'to sign me off on the Rupert Penrith affair which they've punted into the long grass.'

'Oh yes – '

'In the course of her call she pretty much hinted – well, she said outright – that the good folk down in Cheltenham with their sharp little ears may well have put us on their "to do" list and been earwigging our chat.'

'Oh that's absurd. It's flat out paranoid.'

'That's what I said. But she said not necessarily. It's all robotic now, you know, so they can keep tabs on you online. It's not so much what you say as that they can pinpont where you are – God! Look at that idiot cutting in there.'

'White van man.'

'Bloody nearly written-off white van man. Anyway, you and me. Let's keep our sweet-nothings to our own very personal line.'

'You can be Pyramus and I'll be Thisbe. Although look how they ended up.'

'That's precisely because they screwed up their logistics.'

Ginny shrugged.

'OK,' she said. 'We'll talk dirty in private.'

The as and the when, DI Carter confirmed when she called back, was to be the Oxford and Cambridge Club at 1.30pm the next Thursday.

'It's in Pall Mall,' she said, 'just around the corner from Dorset Street, so you won't get lost. On the down side you'll need a jacket. And a tie.'

'No problem,' he had said. 'I'll wear my Ardleigh Old Boy one.'

Suitably thus attired, he took the tube to Green Park and then, shoes newly shined to boot, turned the corner of the Ritz to walk this bright as a button day down St James's towards the Palace and the western end of Pall Mall. Using the zebra crossing to halt the streaming traffic he crossed the broad street to its southern side and within seconds found himself outside his destination. His timing was faultless. He all but bounded up the half-dozen or so stone steps that carried him between the two Union Jacked pillars flanking the notional portico before the club's two-leafed doorway. He was precisely two minutes ahead of the one-thirty witching hour ordained him for this off-beat encounter.

He found himself in a small lobby-vestibule. To his left was a tall reception desk. Behind the desk stood a young, fair-haired woman in the no-doubt-mandatory livery of a sub-fusc black two-piece suit. She smiled enquiringly as he approached her.

'My name is Shaw,' he said. 'I have an appointment with Adrian Wainwright-Smith.'

'Ah yes,' the girl said, 'he's expecting you. Your colleague is already here.'

She nodded firmly in the direction of the wall behind his back. Instinctively he turned. Immediately opposite the reception desk was a fireplace, the grate made tidily up but not lit. To the right of the fireplace was the shallow, token impression of an alcove. Sitting there was DI Carter.

'Ah yes,' he said to the receptionist, 'thank you very much.'

'Mr Wainwright- Smith should be along at any minute, if you'd be kind enough to wait.'

He smiled more thanks and moved across the lobby.

'Sorry,' he said to DI Carter, 'I was looking the other way when I came in: missed you completely.'

'You're not the first,' she said. 'But no harm done. How are you?'

'Fine, thanks. And you?'

'OK-ish,' she said. 'A bit unnerved by all this inactivity.'

There was no other chair to hand so he stood alongside hers. She too was dressed 'sensibly' – another jacket and skirt suit, navy blue in her case, and a cream blouse. No jewellery but a good bag.

They agreed that it was good weather for the time of year.

'Have you got over the screaming ab dabs from the other day?' she ventured.

'I think so, touch wood. Sleeping all night, anyhow.'

'Good. Glad to hear it. You get used to this sodding about waiting when called in by alleged top brass. It all comes under the "let them stew in their own juice" heading.'

'Self-importance likes to make mountains out of molehills.'

'A pretty bloody molehill, mind you. Two molehills actually.'

'Any minute' turned out to be a rather long ten. DI Carter and Ethan spent them inventing things to say and watching the comings and goings in the lobby. Inwards and outwards there was a lot of traffic. A dozen or so young men, barely out of their teens, it seemed, passed hurriedly in and out clutching laptops and iPads fast to the extravagantly knotted ties complementing their expensively off-the-peg suits.

'The eager beaver catches the worm,' DI Carter summed up.

Far slower was the parade of not a few Colonel Blimp lookalikes and an even greater number of sports-jacketed, be-cardiganed fifty or sixty year olds looking faintly lost away from their research papers. They must use the club's restaurant as a canteen, Ethan surmised. There seemed few decidedly middle-aged men. The truly heavy-hitting movers and shakers must be up the road in Whitehall's more powerful corridors. He hadn't spied a single woman.

He took to analysing his surroundings. In a room behind the chimney breast there seemed to be a self-service cloakroom. Beyond the reception desk was a doorless doorway from which people – on one occasion two sweaty youths in squash gear – irregularly appeared. He concluded that over the years the premises had been mucked about a lot – adjoining eighteenth-century town houses acquired en masse and then knocked through and probably extended upwards and to the rear. He looked at his watch. Each time the street door opened he expected it to be Adrian Wainwright-Smith. Each time he was wrong. He and DI Carter continually rated no more than a single, dismissive, passing glance. Well, he'd give it five more minutes.

'What do you think?' he said.

'Give it another five minutes, shall we?' DI Carter answered.

'Ah!' the receptionist exclaimed.

From the doorless gap behind her desk whence, not from the street outside where he might have had some reason for being late, a thus indicated Wainwright-Smith materialised. In a fast, bossy clip, he trotted across the lobby. He came straight over to Ethan, his hand stretched forward.

'DI Carter?' he enquired.

Ethan swivelled sideways and gestured downwards and to his side.

'Ah,' Wainwright-Smith said by way of apology. He took a firm step forward and clasping DI Carter's hand as she rose, impeded her getting to her feet.

He was a poulter pigeon of a man. Plump, and short rather than tall. He had a round face, the face of a disconsolate Pickwick. His most conspicuous feature was his skull and ludicrous comb-over. From the top of a deeply furrowed forehead a broad expanse of utterly smooth, totally hairless scalp extended backwards to the centre and top of his skull. This baldness was halted abruptly by the forward edge of a skull cap made up incongruously of his own black, probably dyed, hair. From a parting positioned so close to his left ear as to risk being taken for a pencil, his brillianteened hair was trained all the way across to the right side of his head. A tall man could have got away with it. At five-foot eight, Wainwright-Smith didn't have an earthly.

He turned now towards the guest he knew not to be a police inspector.

'Then you must be Ethan Shaw,' he said.

'Yes.'

'Curious name, Ethan Shaw.'

'Well, it's short, Mr Wainwright-Smith.'

'Indeed. Shall we go up?'

Their host's abrupt turning to lead the way made clear 'going up' involved ascending the broad marble staircase that rose steeply from the vestibule's rear. An unsightly, eyeball-searing crimson carpet covered the steps which proved positively awkward to negotiate, so steep were their pitch. On reflection, however, Ethan appreciated that the carpet, although strident, was the lesser of two evils. Left bare the staircase would have seemed to be providing a show-casing opportunity, not for Gene Kelly, but Morecambe and Wise.

The three of them made it unscathed to a generous landing. Ahead was another staircase. To the right, though, was a large opening out of which came the distinctive meat and potato aromas of a very British luncheon menu.

'This way then,' Wainwright-Smith ordered rather than urged. His clipped, upper-crust speaking voice had the ability to seem both unctuous and brusque simultaneously. He now employed it conversing with a headwaiter type hovering alongside a lectern just within the wide opening to the club's restaurant. As the two guests waited just short of the threshold, dialogue ensued. Then, brandishing a bound document, the headwaiter led them into the dining area and to a table.

The restaurant was large in area, about the size of a tennis court. Very high ceilinged, it stretched back from very tall windows at the building's front to matching windows in the rear. At the room's dead centre a long oval table was positioned; it was now neither occupied nor covered other than by a low floral arrangement. The remainder of the floor space was filled by rectangular tables set for four. About three quarters of these places were occupied by busily munching members. From the wainscoted side walls portraits of worthies from the previous century gazed anonymously down upon their lunching successors. Their expressions, Ethan summed up in a glance, were as muddied in conception and execution as their over-laying varnish had become.

His party was now being asked to thread its way past most of these latter-day eaters towards the relatively unoccupied area against the further wall. Most of the members were well into their desserts. The headwaiter indicated one of the further tables in particular and smoothly helped DI Carter into the chair he had positioned for her. She was one of perhaps three women present in the entire room.

'We'll be out of the way here,' Wainwright-Smith said. 'Out of earshot. Advantage of starting late.'

As the two men sat Ethan belatedly realised that Wainwright-Smith had also made an effort to dress suitably for the occasion. He was wearing a double-breasted suit in dark blue that had a faint stripe woven into its flannel. It was the sort of suit you might wear in a dock. Where Wainwright-Smith had erred in his dandyish solipsism, however, was in his choice of shirt. Its pattern was made up of adjoining vertical stripes of dark and light blue. Oxford and Cambridge indeed. The grosser error, however, lay in the shirt being topped by a plain white collar unrelated to its body. Given this assault on your visual sensibilities, who would want to enquire as to what membership of what institution the shields on the dark tie were intended to convey? The double-breasted cut of the suit, of course, did no favours at all for the pot belly.

Ethan began to relax. He had vaguely expected to be greeted by some languid-seeming lounge lizard, relatively young and type-cast from spy-thrillers, one whose lazy off-handedness would cloak the dagger of a steel-trap mind. If the powers that were had assigned somebody as unprepossessing as Wainwright-Smith to mark the cards of interlopers blundering upon *l'affaire Khalid Nahkla*, they couldn't be attaching that much importance to it. He wasn't in that deep.

In a sudden flurry four waiters, two male, two female, all young and Asian, had swooped down on the table. The superfluous fourth cover was whisked away and large menus distributed with a flourish. He studied the runners and riders. Yes, English hotel cooking to a fault. To his right DI Carter was already ordering lamb cutlets, Wainwright-Smith – you could have bet your house on it – steak and kidney pie.

'What's the soup of the day?' he asked his immediate waitress.

'Celeriac and Stilton,' she said.

'Yes. I'll have that, please,' he said.

'And to follow?'

'I'll have the fish,' he said.

'Very good, sir.'

She was gone. The headwaiter was returned. The bound document he carried as his symbol of authority was a wine-list.

'The house red here punches a good weight,' Wainwright-Smith said quickly. 'Quite a nifty Shiraz. All right, everyone?'

'Well, since I'm having the bream,' Ethan said, 'perhaps I could have a one-off glass of Muscadet ... '

Wainwright-Smith looked daggers at him from across the table. He was a man whose eyes looked exactly as his voice sounded.

'Of course,' he managed to say.

The starters arrived. The soup was excellent. Both DI Carter and Wainwright-Smith had opted for the melon. Wainwright-Smith looked up from his.

'So you're the painter chappy?' he snapped across the table.

'Give or take,' Ethan said.

'That gives you a decent living?'

The uncouth bastard. DI Carter had thought so too.

'That remains to be seen,' Ethan temporised with. 'It's less than a year since I left Art College. So far, so good, bar one or two little local difficulties.'

Wainwright-Smith was looking puzzled.

'You seem quite old to be just out of college,' he said.

'That's what everyone says. But I was a mature student. A late beginner.'

'Ah. What were you before?'

'I was in the Army.'

'Ah! What regiment?'

'The Service Corps.'

Wainwright-Smith's piggy eyes grew opaque as he lost all interest. However he persisted.

'What rank were you on retiring?'

'Corporal. I didn't privately consider I was non-commissioned officer material, so I quit.'

DI Carter flashed him a grin. Wainwright-Smith returned to his melon.

Their main courses were duly served. The bream was good too and the Muscadet hit just the right spot. For a short while all three of them munched away in silence. The headwaiter-sommelier replenished the red wine glasses. Wainwright-Smith seemed somehow to get more than his fair share. Yes, there were broken veins either side of his stubby nose. He should have made better use of his napkin.

'Right,' Wainwright-Smith abruptly came out with. 'As I indicated, I thought we'd make a late start today so we could end up having the room to ourselves. Which we now pretty much have. I think we can talk quite openly right here and now without having to ferret out some dingy bolt-hole upstairs.'

'Talk about what?' DI Carter said flatly.

'Whom,' Wainwright-Smith declared, 'about whom. About a gentleman of whom all three of us what and whom for present purposes I shall dub with the codename Abenazar.'

'Oh him,' DI Carter dismissively threw away.

'He may come from a totally different world to world to us,' Wainwright-Smith went on, 'but we have to take him seriously. As far as Her Majesty's Government is concerned, and in particular the Foreign and Home Offices, he's a rather favoured alien and as such a worthy recipient of certain privileges.'

'To the Foreign and Home Offices, perhaps,' DI Carter said, 'but not necessarily Scotland Yard.'

'That's almost the whole point of our meeting today,' Wainwright-Smith said smartly. 'Whatever axes Scotland Yard may have, or thinks it has, to grind against Abanazar, in the national interest they have to be laid aside. Abanazar is one of the very few Arab opinion-formers at large in the world today who inclines favourably toward the United Kingdom. As opposed, even, to the United States. You are surely aware to what great extent the UK is reliant upon Middle Eastern oil. Many wily characters have fingers and thumbs itching to turn off the taps on pipelines still, as yet, flowing in our direction, or to throttle the Straits of Hormuz bottleneck still tighter at our expense. We need every friend at court we can muster these days in the Kingdom, in Iran, in Kuwait.'

'If we'd treated certain people better in the past, more fairly,' DI Carter said, 'we wouldn't have to handle Abanazar with kid gloves now and turn a blind eye when he takes the law into his own hands.'

Wainwright-Smith glared at her.

'In a sense that's irrelevant now,' he said. 'Yes, we may have inherited the sins of our forefathers but we have to deal with that inheritance by soldiering on. Abanazar's great virtue for us now is that while he knows everybody, can talk to the highest decision makers in every land, he's unofficial. He allows us to engage in dialogue to pretty much anyone beneath the radar. That gives us wriggle room. Let's say the Saudis are responsible for actions in the Yeman the rest of the world disapproves of. The UK won't want to seem out of step with said rest of the world, naturally. You cannot but be aware our arms industry is hugely dependent on its sales to the Saudis of state-of-the-art weaponry. In a situation like that Abanazar can keep channels open, contacts renewed, and no third party nation need be any the wiser.'

'So therefore the bottom line,' Ethan said, 'is that over here, as a quid pro quo, we permit him to get away with murder.'

Once again Wainwright-Smith pursed his lips the better to unleash his big scowl.

'Rupert Penrith was a British subject,' Ethan continued. 'Not a very nice one in my opinion but you're a British citizen too. If you should be found dead on a Millbank pavement with a scimitar buried in your back, are we supposed to turn a blind eye to that as well?'

'That, as you well know,' Wainwright-Smith said, 'is a perfectly childish hypothesis.'

'So you hope. It makes a perfectly valid moral point.'

Wainwright-Smith altered the direction of his stare but not its intensity.

'Another factor in play as regards Abanazar,' he said, 'is

Israel. Israel, as the world knows, has become something of a loose cannon in the Middle East. A loaded cannon. A nuclear power, let us not forget. The Israelis are hand-in-glove with Washington but hardly so with London. Abanazar is known throughout the Middle East as a passionate supporter of the Palestinian cause. He dearly wants, has everywhere campaigned for, our tribe of Benjamin friends vacating the West Bank, surrendering the Golan Heights. So – when Shylock and Co start getting too uppity for *our* peace of mind, it's very advantageous for us to use Abanazar as a stick to beat some Jews with – for us to make sure they know he's been dropping in to Number Ten of late, as it were.'

'That must make him popular in Tel Aviv,' Ethan said, 'if he's not a double agent.'

Wainwright-Smith let out his breath in an exasperated snort.

'Look, coming right out with it,' DI Carter said, 'I don't know why the fuck your boss or bosses stuck you with getting us here for this mickey-mouse din-dins. They know, we know and you know, that you'd never stand up in court and admit you said any of what you just have said, bloody obvious though it is. And – no, let me finish! – everyone knows the Penrith investigation has already reached the cold case stage – probably in Guinness Book of Records time. Like Penrith himself, it's dead and buried. Nor, in fact, although we have every idea of what happened, do we, to tell the truth, have a shred of hard evidence about it that will hold up in court. There's bugger-all that I or the police in general can do further with it. Your international messenger boy is safe as houses. And as I personally have a desk-load of other crimes to get on with, I'd like to put on record that I deeply resent having my time wasted on such tripey nonsense as this. It's an insult to what I do – ought to be doing. It's an insult to the force.'

Wainwright-Smith had sucked his thin lips in. His cheeks had gone very white. It had been a very long time, Ethan realised, since he had been spoken to like this. But DI Carter had very cleverly given him his out. He knew he could report back that all was well. He was safe. So, then, unless he were utterly vindictive, was she. Wainwright-Smith was reaching into his inner breast pocket now, was dragging out a folded sheet of paper. There was typing on it. Some kind of an *aide memoire.*

'As a matter of fact it's not the Metropolitan Police that causes any concern,' he said. 'Obviously their relationship with the Home Office is always amicable. It's our friend here, Mr Shaw. It would appear that in his own small way he has demonstrated himself to be another sort of loose cannon. Hence the request he join us today.'

I'm sitting here opposite you, you fart, Ethan thought. Give over the third person. He watched as Wainwright-Smith consulted the typed notes and then condescended to look at him directly.

'Am I correct in thinking that in the past Abanazar purchased one of your works?' Wainwright-Smith said in his best schoolmaster. 'Is so to speak, a patron of yours?'

'People do try to patronise me from time to time,' Ethan said. 'It doesn't always work.'

'But he did buy one of your pictures?'

'Paintings. Yes. He in effect commissioned another. A portrait of himself.'

'So it's conceivable he might well get in touch with you again?'

'Conceivable, yes. But unlikely. We didn't part on the

friendliest of terms the last time that we met.'

'I trust I have made it clear that were he to approach you a further time, it would be very unwise of you to do other than refuse whatever offer he might make you.'

Ethan struck the table top in a spontaneous outburst of anger that rattled the cutlery on the spent plates.

'I'm free, white and self-employed,' he said. 'If I did say "no" to an offer I shouldn't refuse, I'd be nothing but a fucking idiot, wouldn't I? Defence of the Realm Act or no Defence of the Realm Act. And didn't you just make it clear we're all supposed to cosy up to him?'

He was vaguely but increasingly aware that behind him the waiting staff were massing as a prelude to clearing the table. Wainwright-Smith's glance seemed to take this in. Visibly he contained his self-importance.

'Well, if he did,' he said, 'we'd expect to hear all about it.' Unexpectedly, he smiled. Ethan realised it was the smile of a man who believes his mission has been accomplished.

'Let's say all's well that ends well,' Wainwright-Smith said. 'However many expletives. Now, then – some pud?'

'Oh for fuck's sake, no,' DI Carter snarled. 'Why don't you just ask for the bill so we can fuck on out of here. And they can too. The waiters. They've been waiting to go for hours. And you, you jobsworth – thank you for nothing. Come on, Ethan, let's go somewhere and get a decent drink.'

As if on automatic pilot, DI Carter led the way across Pall Mall, westward a short distance and then, disconcertingly, had darted into a narrow alley-cum-passageway that was abruptly just there to her right. Buildings rose up on either side – shops, a restaurant, a tailor's – high enough in the direction of a slit of light to create a tunnel effect. About forty yards along from the Pall Mall pavement was a pub. Ethan perceived that The Red Lion had downsized and migrated.

DI Carter led the way inside. It was indeed a rather small space, low-ceilinged, yellow-gold with its parchment-shaded lights and zinc-countered bar, but, thankfully, at this in-between mid-afternoon hour almost empty.

'Now,' DI Carter said, 'what's best to wash that little shit out of our throats and minds?'

'I think I'll go for a Pils,' Ethan said.

'Good shout. I think I will too. No. Let me. I dragged you in on this. Have it on expenses.'

She went up to the counter.

'Two Pils, please,' she ordered.

The twenty-something barman jerked the tops off the two bottles he'd lifted from the cold shelf and, banging them down on the counter in front of her, announced an exorbitant price in a voice proclaiming he came from somewhere between Freemantle and Brisbane.

'For that kind of rip-off we get glasses,' DI Carter snapped.

The barman glowered but said nothing. Stooping, he fetched up two glasses from below his side of the counter. He plonked them down beside the bottles. DI Carter's hand shot forward and she had grabbed the nearer glass.

'Glasses that aren't red hot because they're fresh from the dishwasher,' she snapped again.

This time the barman seemed inclined towards speech, but before his mouth could engage with his brain, DI Carter had slapped down on the zinc counter some sort of plastic-covered card she'd fetched up from her handbag like a gunslinger. The barman took one look at this and remained mute. He turned on his heel and went through a door to the side of the optics. When he returned he was carrying two more glasses. He put them down on the counter rather gingerly.

'You want I should pour?' he asked in Oz.

'I can't afford it,' DI Carter said

The inverted glasses atop each bottle, she came over to Ethan.

'All power corrupts,' she said, 'but police power – don't go there.'

His glass, sure enough, was ice-cold. He carefully poured his Pils into it.

'Cheers,' he said, 'and well done.'

'Cheers. Ah! That's more like it. Well, we certainly know what opinion the Secret Service has of you and me!'

'How – '

'Deputing an obscene jobsworth like that to mark our cards.'

'He certainly did manage to combine being utterly underwhelming with maximum repulsiveness. I've no real idea right now where he – or they – are coming from.'

'Who cares?' DI Carter said. 'Look, it's likely, barring the biggest coincidence, that you and I will never see each other again, isn't it?'

'True.'

'So perhaps for that reason and so you can understand why I found that creep particularly loathsome, I'm going to tell you a secret I don't often – ever, in fact – broadcast around at work.'

'Oh?'

'My first name is Rebecca.'

'Hello, Rebecca.'

'My surname – before I got rather briefly married – was Aspis. Rebecca Aspis, therefore. I'm half-Jewish. It was my father, you'll deduce, who provided the Jewish half. He came to England as late as 1939 on the very last Kinder Transport train to get out of Prague. My mother came from Wigan – from right off the end of the pier, she used to say.'

Rebecca Carter paused to drink and, possibly at a happy memory, smile for a moment.

'My father wasn't orthodox or practising,' she went on. 'He never went to the synagogue. He never mentioned being Jewish – except once. He told me once – and I've never forgotten this – that if a Jew in England tells an acquaintance or neighbour that he is in fact, a Jew, the relationship between the two of them will be profoundly altered.'

'How so?'

'Well, if the neighbour is the one in ten shit that we all come across from time to time, the aforementioned shit, no matter his inferior IQ and qualifications – or lack of same – will automatically hold you in contempt and think himself your superior.'

'Member of the master-race.'

'Of course. But the Jew just can't win, you see. Because, if he tells the nine out of ten decent bloke of a neighbour, then what?'

'I don't know. What?'

'The Jew knows that in any conversation he will subsequently have with him, the decent bloke will be straining every nerve in his brain to demonstrate that he's fair-minded, sympathetic, tolerant. It becomes impossible for the Jew ever to have an objective conversation with the good guy that isn't self-conscious.'

'I'm not sure that's true.'

'No-one ever twigs that I'm partly Jewish because I was brought up in Chorley and sound like I'm straight out of

Coronation Street. And I use my very English married name for working purposes. But when I was at school the nickname they gave me was "sheeny girl".'

'Charming.'

'And, as I said, I don't let on. Not because I'm ashamed or anything – I mean, my life, who's got all the brains? No, I don't let on because of that way it muddies the waters. Like I said the truth of why I've mentioned it to you now is to make clear how pissed off I've been made to feel by that tight-arsed repository of out-of-date prejudice, Wainwright-Smith.'

'I'm not so sure about the tight-arse.'

'I'm glad you said what you said.'

'You said it too. Not your best career move, I imagine.'

'Oh my career's past praying for. I glass-ceilinged out three years or so ago. Just hanging on in for my pension, now'

'Well, we're a nation of multi-cultural, multi-ethnic prejudices, aren't we now? Black, Arab, Muslim, Jew – how do you not feel paranoid?'

'I hope you don't think I'm paranoid.'

'No, not at all. "Paranoid" implies an irrational fear or prejudice. Your reaction to Wainwright-hyphen-Smith suggests very sound reasoning. How should we describe him? He's – '

'A white-supremacist, racist, sexist, irrationally full of himself, essentially an ill-educated, smarmy chateau-bottled prick.'

Ethan grinned.

'I hear he always speaks well of you,' he said.

Rebecca Carter grinned back. Evilly.

'Who cares?' she said. 'His opinions are water off any card-carrying feminist's back.'

'Here's a thought,' Ethan said, 'You were nice enough the

other day to congratulate Ginny and me on being engaged.'

'Yes. Glad to. Happier still to do so again face to face.'

'Well, here's the thing. It's going to be a registry office do. We'll need witnesses.'

'In my line of work you need them all the time.'

'I don't want to bribe any old passers-by at the time to come in and do the business. How'd it be if you did the job?'

DI Carter smiled without a trace of anything other than pleasure.

'Of course it would mean we'd have to meet again.'

'If you're buying the beer that will be ace,' she said. 'You'd've made a good cop.'

16

HE HAD PAINTED THE TABLE-CLOTH a just discernible off-white. That gave him interesting problems when it came to indicating the reflected up-light on to Ginny's dress and neck but it did much subtly to isolate and so emphasise her pose. It required him now to paint an unobtrusive still-life on the cloth. Wine glasses, perhaps, or something salady ... a hint, maybe, of her partner's starter in the immediate foreground ... He was considering the options when, startling him, his mobile trilled.'

'Hello?' he said.

'Ethan Shaw?' a voice so suavely liquid he had no trouble identifying its owner at once.

'Ah,' he said, 'The Red Shadow's shadow.'

'The very same.'

'I trust you back-filled that mock grave and left everything neat and tidy.'

'Of course. Always leave Nature as you found her.'

'Were you planning on dropping in again? You know where to find me.'

'Oh not at all. That's all so much blood under the bridge. I'm actually calling on behalf of Mr Nahkla who – '

'Is unfortunately out of the country at present.'

'How could you have possibly guessed that?'

'Just a shot in the dark.'

'He asked me to ask you if you could countenance remaining on speaking terms with him.'

A good question. Ethan, phone in hand, stood considering it. Master and servant were oleaginous to a fault. Was he really prepared to persist in suffering the insufferable gladly? No, thank you very much. But! It had come to him how much renewing the acquaintance would get up Wainwright-Smith's pudgy nose And there might be a bob or two in it.

'Possibly,' he temporised with. 'Why would that be an issue?'

'I believe he may wish to commission a further painting from you. He admires your work, you know. He likes you. Would a new work be a possibility?'

'Possible, yes. It would depend exactly on what he has in mind. We could talk.'

'That's what he was hoping.'

'But he's abroad.'

'He's due back soon. Briefly. Does the place name Kidlington mean anything to you?'

' ... it rings a very faint bell.'

'It's just north of Oxford. Not so very far from London.'

Overnighting in the industrial unit had not been such a pain after all. The place had a loo and the microwave he'd installed earlier. And the previous afternoon he'd spent an incisive couple of hours in Shepherd's Bush buying an inflatable mattress, a sleeping bag and a duvet. Bringing his usual pillow along with him later, he had slept like a top, snug as a bug in a barracks. All this scurrying about, this nocturnal exiling, had been occasioned by Ginny experiencing an atypical fit of morality.

'Ethan,' she had said, 'I think I have to inflict some bourgeois prudishness on you. If Imogen and Cordelia are going to come up and join us on Friday, I think it would be better, taking the long view, if they didn't find you already ensconced in residence.'

It didn't take him long to take that on board.

'Makes sense,' he had said. "Who's been sleeping in your bed, auntie?" We don't want to puzzle or shock them with our lack of respectability. And I can easily camp out while they're here – an unexpected benefit – around the corner at the studio.'

'Will you be all right there?'

'Perfectly. Better than your average army hut.'

So it had proved. Nevertheless, as he found himself the following evening walking up the garden path of what was again solely Ginny's home, he detected an anxiety in himself he would have thought better located in the breast of a juvenile suitor calling at the dwelling place of the daughter he was hoping to propose to. As arranged – strangely, it seemed – he rang the doorbell. He heard no steps, but the door opened. There stood Ginny.

'Right on time,' she said.

'They here?'

'Yes, no problems at all.'

As she had originally, and not so long ago at that, Ginny led him down the hall and into the all-purpose lounge-living room. As he came through its door two young girls rose to their feet. Score one at least for the headmistress, he fleetingly felt.

'Imogen, Cordelia, this is my friend Ethan,' Ginny said. 'Ethan, that's Cordelia over there and Imogen's here by me.'

'Hello,' he said smiling and looking from one to the other.

'Hello,' they replied pleasingly not quite in unison.

He took them in more slowly. Cordelia, the younger one, took after her biological father: that was to say she was going to be beautiful. She already had a long slender nose, perfectly proportioned to her long, thin face and her wide, back-curving mouth. Her long, blonde hair, parted on one side, hung straight down to frame the face and its fairness made the vivid blue of her eyes border on the outrageous. Imogen was sturdier, promising, if she was only nine, that she would grow up tall and powerful. Her face was rounder than her sister's, her cheerful mouth fuller. Her hair was an eye-catching helmet of natural curls, avoiding any Shirley Temple cuteness by their casual, yet somehow co-ordinated, haphazardness.

'Are you the one who paints things?' Imogen was asking.

'That's right,' Ethan said. 'Things and people. Perhaps one day I might paint you two.'

Pleased to be thought worthy of such a distinction, the girls twisted at their waists to look at each other.

'Ginny says that you and she are going to get married,' Imogen said.

'Yes. That's right too. She will be Mrs Shaw then. I expect that after we are married I'll come and live here. I expect you will too.'

The girls looked at each other in bemusement.

'There's this thing they call adoption,' Ginny said. 'It's for children like you – orphans. It means when children no longer have their first mummy and daddy other grown-ups can come along and take over – take their place. We have to sort it all out with the authorities – the people who look after matters like this – but when we've done that, you two can come here and Ethan and I will be your new parents.'

The two girls' eyes had been getting rounder and rounder, bluer and browner.

'Hermione Gascoine is adopted,' Cordelia said.

'Does that mean we'd give up going to Brookhurst?' Imogen said, hope catching in her throat.

'Oh yes,' Ginny said quickly, 'you'll go to a school round here. A day school – you'd go there during the day and in the afternoon come back here to your home and your own beds.'

'Oooh!' Cordelia said.

'So you can help us with our homework?' Imogen said.

'If you explain it to us,' Ethan answered. He looked at the pair of them. A big ask. A huge responsibility, an ongoing obligation, signing up to raise and cherish two already half-grown souls whose previous lives were already filled with dark happenings. What the hell, he silently thought, go for it: if you can survive being walked to your grave with a gun in your ribs, you can bring up grizzly bear cubs. Yes, go for it!

17

THERE WAS A RUNWAY OF SORTS, large Quonset-type huts housing planes, a control tower, such as it was, but the facility at Kidlington could scarcely lay claim to the title of airport. Air-strip was all it might hope to be thought of, Ethan decided as he slotted his Toyota home in the general car park. There were flocks of planes similarly parked to the further side of the runway and others apparently being serviced inside two of the open-doored Quonset hangars but none of these aircraft looked more bulky than his car. Bi-planes, single-winged, they all gave the impression of being 'sports' planes – the expensive playthings of enthusiasts who no doubt got a bang out of flaunting their riches aloft and talking it up big when their associations and clubs congregated in the bar. Apart from catering for air-taxis and the private aircraft of top golfers, jockeys and those business executives for whom time was serious money, Kidlington was no Heathrow, Gatwick or even Stansted. Essentially a complex of one-storey buildings, it lacked the assembly of hotels, shopping malls, arrival and departure lounges that give the big commercial airports their pervasive sense of blighted city centres. It was late afternoon going on evening. As he travelled the quite long trek from the car park to the low run of administrative buildings, Ethan saw lights blink on in the distance. He heard metal clang on metal and workers shouting with unnatural clarity through the still evening air. He felt himself to be stepping back in time. He was revisiting the site of an early British RAF film.

No Starbucks, then, no Pret A Manger. But Ali had said there was a canteen, a café of sorts, where they might meet. Strangely unchallenged, ignored, in fact, as he negotiated drab corridors through the linked buildings, he eventually pushed open a door to enter into what had to be the place Ali had specified – a low-ceilinged but clean and cheerful double room containing a dozen or so tables covered with brightly-chequered cloths. There was a self-service counter and he ordered a tea and a slice of walnut cake. He sat down to make his table the fourth one occupied and came to the conclusion he could get to like the place. It had the feel of a well-run pop-up café somewhere on the south coast.

He was halfway down his cup of tea when the door opened again and his old friends Ali and Abu walked in. As ever they were immaculately dressed – this time, however, in non-matching leather blouson jackets both visibly sumptuously soft. Ali was wearing a roll-neck sweater beneath his, Abu a polo shirt. Both of them carried bags in either hand – Ali two matching tote bags in leather probably as supple as his jacket's, Abu a bright aluminium suitcase and the ultra-thick attaché case favoured by pilots. They came immediately to the table next to Ethan's and set their luggage down on the floor around it. Ali casually nodded in the direction of Ethan's cup.

'Care for another?' he asked.

'Thank you, I'm fine,' Ethan replied.

Ali went to the counter. In due course he returned carrying two cokes partially poured into glasses.

'Just not the same over here,' he said, brandishing his own glass.

At that precise moment Khalid Nahkla came through the door. Ignoring his lieutenants completely he came across to Ethan's table. Ethan stood up.

'Have bygones become bygones?' Nahkla said. 'Are we still talking?'

'Provisionally,' Ethan said and – why not? – extended his hand.

'Excellent,' Nahkla said. 'May I?'

He sat down at the table anyway.

'Mr Nahkla?' Ali asked.

'No, nothing for me, thank you,' Nahkla said without turning his head and then, 'Thank you for dragging yourself all this way, Ethan, but I've been enmeshed with some of Oxford's great and not-so-great all day, and any moment now I'm due to take off for Thirsk. However I do have good news for you.'

'Oh?'

'I've talked lately to two of the Ardleigh school governors. They tell me they are delighted with the portrait.'

'Fine.'

'Over the moon, to resort to cliché. I left them convincing themselves they've earned enormous credit in discovering such a promising young talent.'

'And so cheap at the price.'

'Well, that too. They'll be staging an unveiling ceremony, of course. You'll have to come to that. It will mean you will be talked about; name on everyone's lips and all that sort of thing. Won't do you any harm. Now tell me: in the meantime are you prepared to accept another commission from me?'

'Probably. Depending, of course.'

'Of course. Well here's about the size of it. I have a dear friend who at the end of this year turns forty. He happens to be the ultimate example of the man who has everything. How, then, to surprise and delight him on his birthday?'

'Admit to him he's wealthier than you are?'

Nahkla allowed himself one of his thin smiles.

'He's already well aware of that,' he said. 'What I had in mind stems from the fact that, like me, he has a passion for thoroughbred horses. He has recently acquired a two-year-old of outstanding pedigree and hence potential. The most beautiful animal. He has made arrangements to have this colt trained in the Chantilly stables of one of France's most celebrated trainers.'

'Yes? And ... ?'

Again Nahkla smiled.

'Every cloud has a silver lining, we are told,' he said. 'I was put in mind of my faux Stubbs sketch. What better, given the circumstances, surprise could one devise?'

'Given what you've said, probably none.'

'Exactly. Might you be interested?'

'Very much so. I'm likely to trail in down the field a long way behind Stubbs, though.'

'I'm not looking for a second-rate Stubbs but a first-rate Shaw.'

'Then arguably I'm your man. Is Chantilly pretty?'

'Very much so.'

'There might be a case for going to landscape, then, and so to watercolour.'

'That's entirely your department and entirely your decision. It would involve going there, of course.'

'That would just be a bonus.'

'And secrecy will be paramount. We'll have no trouble with the trainer. He and I are on the best of terms.'

Ali, abruptly, was standing at their table. Without speaking he extended the Rolex on his wrist into Nahkla's line of vision.

'I literally have to fly,' Nahkla said. 'Time and his Traffic Controllers wait for no man. Your fee?'

'For the man who already has everything, four thousand,' Ethan said.

'Deal,' Nahkla said. 'Take this as a retainer.'

He was writing a cheque. He ripped it free from its book with the panache of long experience.

'I'll be in touch,' he said as he rose. 'I'm so glad we are back in step together. *À la prochaine.*'

'*Bon voyage,*' Ethan managed in return.

They were going. As he stooped to pick up his bags, Ali looked up and smiled his goodbye.

The tea remaining in his cup was tepid to the point of being undrinkable. Waste not, want not. He finished it off anyway. He folded the cheque and slid it into his shirt pocket. Not so very much of a drive down from London and a very nice little earner on the end of it. Nothing more to keep him here. Time to go home.

Once more unchallenged and ignored he retraced his route through the down-at-heel corridors and out into the open. The twilight was beginning to thicken but the air was fresh and reviving. A tall man ahead of him was also heading towards the car park. Mechanically almost, he began to follow in his footsteps. It felt so good to know that his short-term – even his mid-term – future was mapped out for him.

On instinct he had stopped. From the mid-distance a whining, chuntering, hawking cough had brought him back to the present. A metallic cough. He turned his head. At the side of the further end of the runway from where he stood a chunky helicopter was coming to life. Its blades whirling dervishly, it was still on the ground. The engine noise intensified, rose in pitch, and the whole machine was quivering. It rose upward a few vertical feet, turned on its own axis and then proceeded to rise up and forward at a tilted angle of about forty-five degrees. Thirsk next stop. The rich were certainly different from us. Ethan turned for home again already groping in his pocket for car keys as he started to move on. A slap of cold air cuffed his cheek and a nano-second later the herumping boom of a much larger than life explosion positively hurt his ear drums. He spun around. A hundred feet above where he had last sighted the chopper a rose-orange star-burst flashed in the sky at the centre of a halo of smoke. As his mind rejected the reality of what he was seeing, his eyes looked for other signs of damage. Lesser fires hung, floated, fell in the sky. Dark debris plummeted downward. Animal, mineral, vegetable, who could say? The fiery rose at the epicentre of the explosion had now transmuted to an oily blackness. Offset by the surrounding grey-white smoke, it was now slowly guttering earthwards, a stark and malign exclamation point.

'Jesus!' a voice said, 'They've had another one!'

The tall man. The other side of a Range Rover Vogue he was standing with his back turned as he looked to the far end of the runway. Sirens began to wail. Lamps arced light towards the devastation.

'In five minutes the approach road will be stuffed solid with ambulances, fire engines and police cars,' the man said over his shoulder. 'I'm out of here.'

Tall, broad-shouldered, no push-over. The man turned and

ducked into his car. In that split-instant Ethan's heart stood still.

In the course of his twisting motion the man had momentarily silhouetted himself against the glare of the emergency lighting. He had a unique profile. That unique profile. He was the one virtually without a nose. Beneath the level of where his eyes must be was a scooped, concave nothingness. See that profile once and you would never forget it.

Ethan noted down the Range Rover's licence number as he followed it out of the car park. But they must either have been fake plates or artfully calculated to preserve the car's anonymity because although he meticulously documented the incident and relayed it to DI Carter's e-mail address he never heard tell of it again. The world of the Wainwright-Smiths and his superiors had no doubt made sure silence would prevail.

So. The Angel of Death had taken wing again. And Khalid Nahkla had not. The man had had that class and style. It was by no means entirely logical but, all things considered, he thought it somehow classier not to present the cheque he had acquired not so very much earlier that fatal evening.

18

'HAVE YOU BEEN HERE BEFORE?' ETHAN asked.

'Just the once,' Jean Stafford replied. 'I came down and treated myself to a solo celebration the day I got promoted up to DI level. It was a way of steeling myself against the drink-it-up party I was going to have inflicted on me in the pub that evening by all the colleagues miffed out of their minds because they hadn't copped the opening and all the others looking to suck up to the new boss.'

The pair of them were together again this afternoon at a table in the Fortnum and Mason's restaurant.

'Talking of DI level,' Ethan said, 'what do you hear these days from Rebecca Carter?'

'Nothing. I don't. Not a thing. She's resigned the force.'

'Really!?'

'Yes, really.'

'Well, I can't say I'm entirely surprised.'

And that might explain much.

'I think that Penrith case was the last straw as far as she was concerned,' Jean said. 'Mind you, I don't think she was a particularly happy bunny before it. Word is she's lucked into a job as Security Chief for Slumberland.'

'Slumberland?'

'They've got commercials on the box all the time. They're that big chain of warehouse-type bedding outfits alongside every bypass in the British Isles. You know: "Dream sweet dreams with Slumberland".'

'Oh, yes.'

'I suspect her main job will be to stop more flatpacks going out of the back door than the front.'

'Sounds tedious.'

'But remunerative.'

'So long as she doesn't lie down on the job.'

'Ho, ho,' Jean said. 'But that's not her style. She'll do very well there. Good luck to her.' She looked searchingly across the table. 'In the meantime,' she went on, 'I'm not at all sure why I should be *here* right now. To what do I owe the honour of your invitation?'

'I'll make that clear in due course,' Ethan said.

'Why Fortnum's?'

'No particular reason. Probably because it's so near to the Academy and, as you'll see, that seems vaguely appropriate. What do you fancy?'

'I think I'll be kind to you and go for the cream tea.'

They duly ordered two cream teas.

'And yourself?' he said. 'Are you working on anything interesting?'

'Yes and No. Something routine but worthy. There's a small, early Titian in this country. It was brought here by an Austrian in 1946 just after the war. A mathematician. He had a long and prosperous academic career here and the painting now belongs to his niece. Only it doesn't. We've helped establish that it was looted from a Jewish household in Vienna in the mid-1940s. It rather introduces the probability that the distinguished academic got into the country on the strength of not a few porkies. Some of the Jewish family survived the Holocaust. There are descendants who are thus the rightful owners. Now. Why am I here?'

'Well, to begin with, do you know if it's possible to enter an art work for the Academy's Summer Exhibition posthumously?'

'I don't know. But I shouldn't think so.'

'Pseudonymously, then?'

'Again. I've no idea. Possibly, I suppose. Why do you ask?'

'I managed to park in St James's Square. If, fortified by your tea, you could totter that far, all will be revealed. Can you manage that?'

'It will be better than pounding a beat. Let's go.'

'My gosh!' Jean was able to say in due course, 'Does that thing have an MOT?'

'Certainly ma'am. Until it goes in for its next one,' Ethan said. 'But it's not my noble veteran car that brings us here, it's what's in it. The thing contained not the container. Just stand there a second.'

He went to the rear of the Toyota and sprang the boot open. Inside, stretching the width of the boot and extending forward into the car's interior over the folded down rear seats was a large painted canvas. Unbidden, Jean stepped closer the better to examine it. Ducking her head and stooping sideways, she let out her breath in astonishment.

'Good Lord!' she said, 'How fantastic! Why, it's wonderful. I don't know how to begin to describe it.'

'You can begin by saying that it's big,' Ethan pointed out.

He gently manoeuvered the canvas out from the car and

stood it inclined against the rear bumper. Taller than wide the painting presented the viewer with a vertical. It showed the larger than life head and shoulders portrait of a young man crowding the foreground of the composition to the viewer's left hand. Over the sitter's shoulder – yes, it was in effect a double portrait, you belatedly appreciated – in the generous background stood on an easel at an angle of some forty-five degrees to the viewer a second portrait of the young man. He was wearing identical clothes – a casual, twentieth-century, open-necked shirt – both in the forward, outward-looking study and in the angled likeness on the easel deeper within the frame. In that latter, recessed, so to speak, depiction, his expression was guarded and formal. It was the portrait of a man gravely posing to be painted. In total contrast the outward-looking image was utterly carefree. The subject – surely the artist himself; the further likeness had to be a self-portrait – was caught turning from his handiwork upon the easel to share a moment with an onlooking friend. His mouth was beginning to open in speech, a lock of hair was loose on his forehead, his hazel eyes were bright with hope and full of the joys of life. These bold, dominating features belonged to someone on the edge of life, looking forward in keen anticipation of all the good days to come.

'Wow! It's magnificent!' Jean said. 'He's so alive. It's like a Thomas Lawrence on wheels. Does it have a title?'

'It's called "Self-Respect".'

'It must have taken you for ever.'

'Who said I painted it?'

'Who did, then?'

Ethan nodded at the canvas.

'He did,' he said. 'The model. Kenneth Marsh. It's a very clever self-portrait.'

Straightening up, Jean contrived to look Ethan squarely in the eye while staring at him askance.

'Pull the other one,' she said. 'He never did. I had to trawl through all Marsh's leftovers for the Antiques Roadshow files. This was never among them.'

'He gave this to me the last time I went to see him,' Ethan said stoutly. 'Artist to artist. He was proud of it.'

'No, he never did,' Jean insisted flatly. 'He never had this attack. This is you.'

'Not true. This is him when young.'

'It's you. How did you manage it?'

'OK, you win – between ourselves. I sourced an old photograph from a Royal Academy yearbook. Faded and bland, of course. I concocted the character from knowing him. It's what he might have done then.'

'Better.'

'He was proud of his skills, you know. He hated himself for allowing his talent to get side-tracked. He knew only too well what he had lost by that. That was the real reason he killed himself. This is to redress the balance. You have to admit it's got his mark all over it.'

'I'll give you that.'

'That's why I'd like to submit this to the Academy for the Summer Exhibition – in his name. I thought that, wearing your uniform, knowing people, you would have a touch more clout than I've got. Than I do. It didn't take me all that long actually. He could have done it at my age. I thought someone should give him credit where credit should have been due.'

'Or isn't. You've forged a forgery purporting to be the work of a confirmed double-dyed forger.'

'Not so illogical, if you think about it. It might well be a good example of two wrongs making a right.'

'They don't, though, do they? Not in this case. Almost by definition the last thing a forger can claim to have is self-respect.'

'On the contrary. If his work is hanging in the Museum of Modern Art, self-respect is the only reward open to him.'

'You can't really expect me to enter this for consideration for the Summer Exhibition for you.'

'For him.'

'It's not on.'

'Look – it's an image. A thing. It exists now in its own right. It's either good or not so good. What the hell difference does whose signature is scrawled in the bottom corner make?'

'Everything, if you work for Sotheby's.'

'Bollocks. A rose by any other name smells just as sweet once it's been framed. You came across this during your tidying up operation, didn't you?'

'I ... '

'Look, Jean, do it. Just do it. An old friend once told me that when it comes to looking at paintings from ten feet away ignorance is bliss. So just do it. If it eases your conscience you can submit it as "Portrait of an Unknown Artist as a Young Man".'

Jean Stafford pulled back her shoulders and gave him the most old-fashioned look in her armoury.

'We'll need a cover story,' she said.